ONE LAST SHOT

By
D. J. McAllister

ISBN: 978-0-692-86400-5

Design: Dedicated Book Services, (www.netdbs.com)

DEDICATION

This book is dedicated to all the Military Members, Veterans, First Responders, and Emergency Personnel who save our lives and protect the American People on a daily basis.

Many thanks to Betty, who without her, these books would not have been completed.

If you liked this book please post a photo of this cover on your Facebook account or other social media so your friends and their friends will know where to buy this book.

AMAZON.COM / Books / djmcallister

Contents

FOREWORD

America is a peace loving, God fearing country that was founded by people escaping aggression and hate. These people began a country founded on Christian values and principles. America has always welcomed these kind of people to its shores.

But there are those who wish to tear America down to their level and drag it through the mud. We don't want these people here!

Let me give you a partial list of the kind of people we do NOT want within our country.

Atheists, people who do not believe in God or believe there is no God. We don't want them. Don't come here!

Anti-American, people who don't like America or what it stands for. We don't want them. Don't come here!

Anti-Israel, People who don't like Israel and the Jewish People. That is God's country. Read the Bible!

People who want to do harm to other people for no reason or for what they think is fun. Don't come here!

People who refuse to learn the English language. Don't come here!

People who think all those people who do not agree with them are deplorable and should be killed. We don't want them. Don't come here!

People who praise or worship the Devil. Don't come here!

Communists, jihads, leftist radicals, liberals, Nazis, socialists, we have enough of them already. Don't come here!

We have had people who live in this country tell us, and anyone who would listen to them, that America is not exceptional. They are wrong! It is the most exceptional and best country in the world to live in. But they have not said which county is the best in their mind.

What I do not understand is this. If that is what they truly believe, then why don't they move to that country that they feel is the best and live there? These people have money and they could go today. These people are liars. We don't want them here.

Chapter 1

Cleaning Up The Mess

I've been with the USSS for a few years now and we have been hunting terrorists and crooks the whole time. I started because of some counterfeiters and money laundering. That was a lot of fun. But terrorists and drug dealers seem to have taken all my time since then.

We have chased terrorists for these last several months across several states until we found a way to lure them into a little trap. And it worked.

It was a very long day. It was a long month. Hell, it was a long year, and there's two more months to go! We found and eliminated several gang members, a few drug dealers who were downright uncooperative and three major terrorists. So it was a very good year.

Our Foundation gave away so many cars and trucks, I didn't even try to keep count. I am glad that we found a way to help change the lives of many people who needed a hand up. The best one was the Ranchero that Norm and his crew fixed up and gave to my partner Jim.

It was Halloween day when we had the big party and we caught three terrorists who had infiltrated our political system and they had been causing all kinds of trouble for us. We ended the trouble with a Congressman and a State Representative deciding to join all the folks at Leavenworth and a Governor's Assistant went to the morgue.

We're all still in DC at the Watergate. It took a little doing, but we got all the partiers out of the room. The Metro Police took our terrorist friends to jail and the one to the morgue. Now here we sit. What a strange group we are. All of our team from back home. My FBI contact, Martin Butcher, my two CIA contacts, Robert Olson and Marco (Mark) Garcia, Senator Ray Weatherby, Senator Joe Rodgers, the Speaker of the house, Chuck Johnson, and least of all, Mister PC. I don't even bother repeating his name.

From the CSPD there was, Lieutenant Lopez, Jim, Ann Webster, 2 guards, the MC, waiters, the Maître D, and me. We pulled other tables together to make a huge conference table. One by one all the participants pulled up chairs from all around the room, and sat with us.

The Speaker, Charles Johnson began the questioning.

"So what are you going to do now?" He said looking at me.

"Well, since we have a terrorist who was from Colorado, we are going to scrub the state of all the dirt we can find." I said. "You guys are lucky. You've got one that's still alive. All we have is a body in the morgue, and he won't talk to us. Maybe I should shoot him in the thigh."

That got a big laugh from all who knew me.

"What are you planning?" The Speaker asked.

"We'll start when he entered the country and uncover every detail. He must have had help. We need to know who and how it happened. We don't know where he came from or when. He could have been here for twenty years. Fortunately we have a very knowledgeable staff and we are dedicated in taking our country back from the haters and the killers. If we have to kill them all, we will. Some of us will enjoy that." I smiled a little.

"We should break it all up into manageable bites." Lopez said.

"I have some friends in Missouri, and I know they would be glad to help." Robert Olson said.

"I have a whole team of friends who wish they were here and will be glad to help. I'll give you phone numbers, or if you want, I'll call Mike McCoy myself. You can have Thomas Wilson as long as you keep him in Leavenworth." I said.

"I'll bet that Thomas Wilson will get the surprise of his life when he enters Leavenworth." Olson said.

"We'll be glad to take the creep from Colorado, Harold Downey. He was a former Assistant to the Governor of Colorado. I'll bet the Governor has already heard and is wanting to talk to us right now."

"And that only leaves James Hardesty, Kansas State Rep, who will also be staying at Leavenworth. My friend Martin Butcher from the FBI has graciously agreed that the FBI will take his case. I gave him Lieutenant Brown and Ted's phone numbers. I'm sure they will help."

When we first got wind of terrorist activity there in the Springs, Lieutenant Lopez put Sergeant Solano in charge of the ones he actually knew about.

"There's a teacher in Boulder who showed up on the background check by Lieutenant Lopez. We found him as a Professor at CU in Boulder. We think he wrote the resumes for two guys and then he had some others write recommendations." The Sergeant said.

"Do you know who he is?" The Speaker asked.

"Yes." Solano said.

Lopez picked up the phone and called back home to his office. Sergeant Solano gave the name and description of the Professor and where the professor could be found to the officer on the phone.

Lopez grabbed the phone back and talked a little louder this time.

"Pick him up! And if he gives you any shit, shoot him!" Lopez said.

Wow, he is fired up! He slammed the phone down. Then looked a little sheepish at what he had done in front of everyone there.

"Terrorist teachers are the lowest form of life there is!" He said.

The Speaker and I and all our guys laughed about that, but the outsiders didn't. That was the first time I ever heard Lopez say a swear word.

I turned and spoke directly to Mister PC. "That was especially for you!"

He scowled a little at that but kept silent. Good!

"I've heard this name, One Shot. Let me think where." Senator Weatherby said.

"It would have been in KC. I spent some time there." I had to laugh again.

"I think it was the VP. Do you know him?" He said.

"No."

"Would you like to meet him"? The Speaker asked.

"Not particularly." It's hard to tell the Speaker of the House, 'No'. I tried, but as you can see, I got nowhere.

"OK, let's go." The Speaker said.

"You aren't listening! Didn't I just say no? I have no interest in politics and any other shuckin' and jivin'."

But we went to the Big House anyway. We met the VP and some others. I made a special disguise back home before we left on this trip just for this kind of thing. I had a feeling that things would go south and I would need one. I have a special one that makes me look like I'm related to that guy on late night TV. You know the one.

It worked. The VP asked if I was related to him and I dodged the question very skillfully.

"Is he Irish?" He was still talking, he never even heard me.

The VP asked if I would like a job in DC.

"NO. I won't work in DC. I would quit first."

"You don't like our town?" He asked.

"Not even a little."

"Why?" He said.

"Too many big shots, no one does anything that they feel seems beneath their stature. I would cut and stack firewood if someone needed it, and I would shovel out a barn if I'm asked to. How many people do you know who will do that?"

He changed the subject quickly. I knew what he wanted from me and I'm not going to give it to him.

"Now I know who you are. You're the one who shot those cartel guys and the gangs. It didn't look like anyone had the balls to take them on. But you did. I see that you are wearing a vest. Do you wear it often?" He asked.

"Every day, all day long."

"Can I see the gun?" He said.

I opened my jacket and showed him but did not take it out.

"You may look but do not touch. This is what I do every day."

The Speaker had an idea to go through halls of congress and ask questions. He said we should get together and write the questions they want answered. We sat down right then and brainstormed ideas for the right questions. I spit some out and he wrote them in 'Staffenese' on his note pad.

"I can't do that! I'm not a member and besides I have no interest in going in there and making a fool of myself. You belong, so it's your job."

"The team can start without you." He said.

"Yes they can, but they won't. My final answer is emphatically NO! We need to hire a few PI's to find the info on these men. Our Private Investigators have been doing the job a long time and they know what they're doing. Besides it will give our people a break in the pressure."

I think he finally saw that my argument was the better one and he agreed, but very slowly.

"We'll need background checks on them all the way back to birth, known associates, friends, relatives, anyone they talked to during business hours and beyond, teachers and students during school." He said.

"Yes! Yes! I know how to do background!"

As we came out of the Big House, we were met by a group of people with cameras and microphones screaming at The Speaker and pushing me out of the way. One guy pushed me and I smacked him.

"Who the hell do you think you are? You can't hit me like that!" He yelled.

"I just did, you terrorist! And I'll rip your head off if you touch me again. Now get out of the way and take your low-life friends with you before I have you all arrested!"

I said it all loud enough for all of them to hear. I didn't want any of them saying that they weren't warned. They all stopped and looked at me and the cameras suddenly were facing me.

He got a shocked look on his face and ran away. Another one yelled at us. "We want an interview!" Another one stuck a microphone up to the driver's door, but he got nothing.

"You are now considered terrorists! I don't speak to terrorists!"

He stopped and looked at me and began to raise him camera up in my face to take my picture. I grabbed the camera and threw it out behind the car onto the paved driveway. It hit with a terrible crashing sound and he almost fainted. I leaned over and looked him in the eye and said. "What did I just tell you?"

The driver had the car waiting and Chuck was already in the back seat. I pushed two more creeps out of the way and entered the back seat and we were off. I'm sure there will be pictures of me on the news very soon.

"Is this the way it is with you every day, Chuck?"

"Usually not this bad, but it is a hassle sometimes." He said. "By the way, I don't think they all were terrorists."

"Good! Because I like to shoot terrorists!"

Later, The Speaker made a special point to get me away from the rest of the people to a place where it was quiet.

"Look, I know your name is not 'OS McCoy' that's some kind of joke." He said.

"No. It's not a joke. Let me explain the 'One Shot McCoy' to you."

I told him the story of 'One Shot McCoy' and how it got started. I explained all about my cousin Mike and his stunts at the range and my one hundred yard shot. I even told him a little about the drug dealers who were eliminated. I explained Amy and the money 'laundry' to him and he finally laughed.

"Do you regularly shoot these drug dealers and the others?" He asked.

"Any time someone pulls a gun on me he can expect that I will pull mine. And if there's one thing I learned in school and the Academy, if he pulls a gun he is ready to use it and you'd better be ready to shoot back. Or in my case, shoot first."

"I have spent a lot of time practicing on the range and in the forest. I don't advertise that and I don't brag about how I can shoot, but I don't waste a shot.

If a guy pulls down on me, I'll shoot to kill with one shot. Don't pull it out if you're not going to use it"

"How many have you shot?" He asked.

"You don't want to know. It's a big number."

I gave the Speaker a card of mine with DJ McAllister, the word 'Author' under the name and a phone number. He examined it like it wasn't for real.

"That's my actual name. One Shot McCoy was just to scare the bad guys. And it works."

After we left the Big House and got back to a quiet place, I asked the Speaker if he would like to visit the house on Happiness Drive. He could meet my family and friends, and kick off the cares of the world for a few days. I told him about the blue plane and he said that he would fly commercial. He added later that he would like to see the plane.

It was good to get home from all the hustle and bustle in DC. I hugged and kissed everyone in the house and we all sat and talked for a couple hours about what we did. The girls were especially interested in all the little details.

Once I got to the office, I put the word out about the terrorist from North Carolina reportedly being in our area. They said he was reported in Pueblo. Lopez received a whisper from someone and he sent three cars down to pick him up. There was a little action, but the guy lived through it. Darn it!

I found that Lopez had already begun assigning jobs to the members of the team. Jim met me at the door and filled me in with the basics.

"Everyone is talking about that guy with The Speaker of the House at the Big House yesterday. We all know that was you. How did you get away with it?" Lopez asked.

"I was just me being me. But it was fun."

"Boy, the Media wants to kill you, or him." He said.

"We have most of it back to normal. There are a few crazy things going on, but that's pretty normal for us." Jim said.

"Good! Let's take a few days off and get back in the Colorado groove. I would love to have a cook out and blow of the DC steam. Whataya think?"

"I'm all for it. Should we tell Lopez?" Jim said.

"Sure. Might as well get everybody involved."

We whispered in Lopez's ear and he jumped out of his chair like he had springs in his legs.

"What a great idea!" He yelled. "Attention!"

Everyone stopped what they were doing and faced Lopez.

"Pot luck at DJ's house tomorrow all day. Bring your fancy foods and we'll wash off the DC dust and get back to work on Monday. See you there." He said.

There was a sigh of relief and a swell of laughter and happy talking immediately and it slowly calmed down as everyone went back to what they were doing. I expect this one might be the best cook-out and fun time we will have all year.

It was like we never left. The women brought the best and fanciest food I have seen in a long time.

Lieutenant Lopez, Jim and I sat in the back and talked business. Lopez and the PD had been working twenty four seven since they returned from DC.

They found a lot of possible leads to teachers and professors. The Springs has a lot of public and parochial schools. We'll look at them later. Our main focus has to be on the schools of higher learning. There are a lot of college level subdivisions and trade schools here.

Lopez had drawn a gridwork over a huge map of the Pikes Peak region on the wall and numbered the squares. Each square has a space for identification for schools and number of terrorists if we find any. We will work one grid at a time and clean it all up if possible.

"You were right about one thing." Lopez said. "There's a note on your desk from the Governor. He wants to see you 'at your earliest convenience'."

I know what that means. I made a call and set an appointment for next week.

Chapter 2

Making A Plan

I was notified a few weeks later that the Speaker was going to arrive at Pete Field on Monday. He would be flying incognito on commercial and they gave me the arrival time and the flight number. At first, I thought he would fly into the small airport at Falcon. But that's what you get for thinking.

I drove my little blue racer when I picked him up. I thought he might enjoy a big to little change. He did.

"This is quite a big surprise. I expected you to show up in a big Lincoln Town Car, not of all things, a Porsche 356." He said.

"A guy has to have a little fun once in a while, and this is it. Where would you like to go? Better buckle up!"

I made it a point to take the corners too fast and to exceed the speed limit when I could. He ate it up.

"Do you really have a house on Happiness Drive?" He asked.

"Of Course."

"And a Foundation, and a Bank? Could I see it? Where did you get the money?" He asked.

"It's a secret, you already know that I have a TS clearance. And I can't tell." I smiled the biggest smile I could. He smiled a little tiny grin. You could tell that it hurt him.

We stopped to see Norm on the way to the house. Norm explained what he did for the Foundation and about how many vehicles he puts out in a month. Norm had his usual load of cars and trucks in work. But he always has one or two hidden in the back. We found a 1948 Ford two door and a well used '52 Chevy.

We stood and talked to Norm and looked at the stuff in his building for a while. Then Norm said to The Speaker, "We all saw you on TV."

"Did you see the funny looking guy with the big mole on his face?" Chuck said.

"Yeah, who was that?" Norm asked.

Chuck pointed with his thumb over his shoulder at me.

"That was DJ?" He said and they both laughed a lot at that.

"It's time to go." I headed for the door. They were still laughing as we went through the door.

I took a shortcut past the bank and only stopped for a minute, so he could get a look at it. It was only a few more minutes before we were walking into the Happiness Drive hovel.

I made all the introductions and both of my girls were just beside themselves, but Harry was unimpressed. He must take after his dad. Denise made it a point to hug Chuck. Ted and Vonnie were there and they smiled and shook his hand. He didn't know who they were. I had to explain it all about Ted and what he did.

"Ted works at Bayer in Kansas City, and they flew out here just to see YOU." I couldn't help but laugh. Then the rest of them did too.

After dinner, we were sitting in the family room downstairs in the nice soft chairs with some drinks and snacks when he began again with the questions.

"What do you write?" He asked.

"Nothing, I can barely write my name. This is just a cover. That's just a card with contact info for you and any important others. I can go anywhere and ask all kinds of questions and say that I'm writing a book and just doing research and no one ever questions me. You would be surprised where I have been as a writer and who I've talked to."

I walked out into the back yard with him and he saw the two garages. "What do you need two garages for?" He asked.

"We have two banks and two girls and two lawyers and two Financial Planners, why not two garages?"

He stopped and stood there laughing. "Are you always like this?" He said.

"What you see is what you get. In answer to your question, let me show you. My wife's car and the one I drive are in that one." I pointed toward the house. "And two special cars are in the other. Come on."

We entered in the side door and he saw my little blue racer. But he had already ridden it that. We walked around it and he got a look at the other.

"What is that?" He said.

"Years ago, I built this for me and my first wife, Sarah. She fell in love with this little car and she drove it everywhere. After the wreck I had this car delivered to my garage where it is now. I couldn't even look at it for a very long time. As you can see, I built a wall in the middle of the garage to block it out of my view."

"Over the years, I worked a little here and a little there to bring the car back to life. I did all the same things that I did when I was building it in the beginning. I bought a hood, fenders and dash from the same company in California. New wheels, tires and all the glass. Most of the wood could be saved."

"I found another VW to use as a donor car. I made all the necessary cuts and installed all the necessary parts and all the wood. Replacing the Porsche engine and transaxle from the wreck into the new VW was a big problem, but Gene was available again to do the most of the hard work."

"Now I have another 1940 Ford VW Two Door Woodie Wagon in original Ford maroon sitting in my garage. Gene and I have tested it and it runs just as well as the first one. He wanted to make sure that it would run a hundred like the other one did, and it does."

"The first time I drove it, I almost felt like Sarah was riding with me. I'll probably always miss her."

The next day we drove out to the airport at Falcon in the Woodie and he got a big shock when he looked at the big blue plane.

"This is yours too?' He said.

"Yes and no. It belongs to the Foundation. We use it to get back and forth to problems or friends. Ted and Vonnie came out in it last weekend."

He looked at it and touched it and, of course, he had to look inside.

Later I took The Speaker to Peterson in the Bank President's car to catch his plane back to DC. I hope we can count on him for the support we will need in this struggle.

Now that The Speaker has left, we can get down to business. Lopez and the rest of the crew have been working their fingers to the bone since they returned from the east.

Lopez decided that he would work on backgrounds on all three of them and if his crew found anything, he would pass it on to the specific crew working that guy.

And naturally he started with the Colorado guy, Downey. One of the ladies in the crew found a nice little tidbit. All three of these creeps were born in Baghdad. They must have known each other, although we haven't found any evidence of that yet.

We worked on all we had for a week and it was time to make a conference call to Mike and Brown.

"Hey Mike this is DJ. Lieutenant Brown, are you on too?"

"Yes DJ, this is Lieutenant Brown."

"I'm here too." Mike said.

"We found a connection to the three guys. Our guy was born in Baghdad and there was a professor at CU, named Richard Johnson, that helped them get into the country. And he did it legally back then. That was about twenty five years ago, though. We haven't been able to locate the professor since we found his name. We don't know if he skipped the country, or if he died, or what happened to him. I already sent you his name and vitals. You got anything?"

"We know that Wilson was born in Baghdad." Mike said.

"So was Hardesty." Brown said. "I wonder if they were related or neighbors. It's so hard to tell now that everything is blown up over there. We need known associates, office assistants, those in other offices, girl friends, family, former addresses."

"We have done all that on Wilson. But get this. Wilson had a girlfriend in KC and Topeka and DC that we know of." Mike said.

"Good! Let's get them too."

"We know that the professor helped all three get a GED and all the first required bits of education that they needed. They picked Journalism, Politics and Law. Ours was the lawyer. They went to CU, KU, and Missouri. Maybe you'll have some luck finding more information on them."

"I don't know if those schools have extensions here, but I'll look into them first thing tomorrow." Mike said.

"Did the Congressman or the other two have people that they met with regularly? Office workers, their friends, other offices, do they go to other offices on the other side? There must be others. They couldn't have done it all by themselves."

"I'll check for rap sheets on both of them." Brown said.

"OK guys. That's all we have for now. Give us a call if you get something. See ya."

Mike stayed on, he had something else to talk about.

I told Lopez. "I know a couple of Private Investigators who would be glad to help us find these guys. One is in Pueblo and one is in Littleton. I'll call them right now."

"You know, I think I can get a couple PI's to help too." Lopez said. "I'll have them check their backgrounds. Known associates, FBI, CIA, local PD's, friends, relatives, business, workplace, teachers, students. You know, all the stuff."

I think the professor helped create a new identity for all three of them. Mike said.

"How do you do that?

"We're still working on that." Mike said.

It was a nice long drive to Denver. I parked in a reserved space in front of the Capital Building and walked in to the receptionist's desk.

"May I help you sir?" She said.

"I'm DJ McAllister. I have an appointment with the Governor."

"Why yes you do. I will ring him for you." She said. "Sir, I have Mr. McAllister here for you now."

"Good! Send him in!" He said.

I can tell by the sound of his voice that this isn't going to be good.

I opened the big oak door and slowly walked into the big wood covered office. He stood and offered his hand to me. I didn't expect that, but I shook his hand and he motioned for me to sit. Which I did.

"I've heard a lot about you DJ. You may be the best cop we've had around here in many years. But you seem to attract dead bodies. I must admit, the work in DC was a phenomenal idea, and it has started a lot of people thinking about new ways to do things." He said.

"Governor, I am very sorry about Downey. None of us knew who was at the head of this terrorist organization. We asked one of them and he gave us the name of a country singer. Which, of course, was another one of their lies."

"I have empowered a team of inspectors to help find these people and rout them out of our state and into a very nice new home for them down near Canon City. Have you ever been inside MAX?" He asked.

"No sir. And if you don't mind, I would rather not go there at all. I have seen the concrete monster in that little town in Kansas, and I visited the State Pen at Canon City once on a tour. That was enough for me."

"All right then. You put them in, and I'll keep them there." He said.

"But the next time you catch someone who is close to any one of us here, please give me a heads-up. I was blind-sided with the news about Downey." He said. "I would have asked you to take his place, but Speaker Johnson told me how you felt about politics."

"Well, politicians aren't allowed to shoot terrorists and I am."

He smiled a lot but stopped and handed me one of his business cards with his private numbers on it.

"I have heard that you have helpers in Missouri and Kansas. I think I can help there too." He said. "By the way, Speaker Johnson had some very glowing remarks about you. It seems you may be one of his favorite people."

Chapter 3

Schooling

I was sitting in front of one of the computer screens with Officer Dave Pearson scrolling through the names of faculty and employees of the colleges when something caught my eye.

"Wait! Stop! Back up! There in the middle of this page. The name!"

"What name?" The officer asked.

"Right there." I pointed to the name on the screen. "Professor William Nelson, Math."

"Do you remember when that guy told us that the General's name was George Jones? I'll bet they listen to our music and try to learn our language. Maybe they think we'll not notice names like country singers and athletes and movie and TV people because they think we are so familiar with them."

"You don't suppose that this Professor William Nelson is a terrorist as well?" Dave said.

"I'll bet if we thoroughly search this register, we will find more like this. They didn't use 'Willie'. Maybe they are trying to disguise it a little. Get some help on this project. I don't want any of them to get away because we weren't on the ball."

He picked up the phone and began talking.

"I think it's worth a very long look." I told him. "Maybe they listen to our radio and they think we won't notice those names. And tell everyone, NO

LEAKS! If this gets into the media, we will lose every one of them!"

Mike called the other day with an amazing story. He got a call from a friend of his working at a nearby college. It seems that some of the students had put up some posters alerting the other students to possibilities of terrorism at the school.

"These posters were anti-terror and there were a few that were pro-Israel since they are a big anti-terror country."

"The next day the posters had been torn down, they were found torn up and stuffed into a dumpster. This kid is really on the ball. He went to get a copy of the security tape, and it clearly showed who the culprit was. He called Mike and they went out and arrested the terrorist and he is presently visiting Leavenworth. The culprit's Professor turned out to be a terrorist also, a friend of Professor Johnson. The prof told him exactly what to do and how to do it. We got him too. But we didn't get Professor Johnson."

Mike continued with another unbelievable story.

"One of the investigators found a pile of notebooks and other books in the bottom of a locker hidden away in the basement of a school in Lawrence. It read like a screen play. Every word, direction and response was recorded."

"Strangely enough, the name on the notebooks was not one of the three terrorists we were investigating. We haven't found the owner of that name as yet, but we will. The date was correct, but the name was not. It looks like there was another person in the room during these first few meetings. But who? Was it one of their people or someone hiding and taking notes? If it was a spy, who were they working for? I've never heard of any of this." Mike said.

"According to the notebooks, the Professor stood and went to the blackboard."

He told them, "You must learn all you can about their politics, law and journalism. Every detail, at every level. This is how we will overcome them."

"You must choose one career and continue to the end of the course. I will provide the right instructors as you go along. Each of you three will go to a different school and finish and graduate with a degree. I will help speed things up if possible." The prof said

"All this we found from papers and notebooks, picked up at random at different places." He said. "The older one, Wilson, came into the country legally about twenty five years ago. The professor found a way to circumvent the law and taught it to Wilson."

"All these courses have a required class called Ethics. They met in Ethics class. They all laughed at the class content and began to espouse their own stupid ideas of terroristic ethics to others. Back then, it wasn't noticed as much." He said.

What we know now is this, there was a professor at CU Boulder that one of them knew and he helped them get into the country. They came separately at different times. He didn't have a country singer's name, so we didn't find him as easily. But we did.

Now that we have found him, it has been tough to get him to talk, but I have a time-honored way of getting them to talk. I'm just waiting my turn. I hope he has strong thighs.

He moved them here about twenty five years ago and they all entered legally. All three of them are in their late forties. My man Downey won't be getting any older though.

All three of them entered a small school where they earned their high school diploma after only a few months. Once the high school was finished, it was time to go to college for one of the three disciplines that the professor had picked out for them.

Downey picked Law, Wilson picked Politics and Hardesty picked Journalism.

Officer Dave whispered to me that he had a few names he wanted me to see. Oh boy! I hope it's a list of names I have seen or heard before.

"You won't believe the names I found in the college listings." He said.

"OK. Let's have it."

"The first one is Alan Jackson. I really want to interview this guy. If he's not tall, blonde, wears a cowboy hat, and can sing, we better give him a good look. Then there's George Jones again, William Anderson and Edward Murphy. They should pick a name that no one has ever heard of, like Ken Wallace." He said.

"Before we start on this, we need to talk to our friends at Leavenworth to see if they will take our 'possibles' for a short stay until they are cleared or not."

I need to call Mike.

"Hey Mike. I have a little job for you that would be a big favor for me."

I explained what I wanted from Leavenworth and Mike said he would take care of it tomorrow.

Mike took a trip to our favorite prison to get all our ducks in a row, but it's done now and we have a secure place to hide our non-friends.

We sent the whole list of possibles to the FBI for a review and after a few weeks, we had some good useful information.

It turned out that Professor William Nelson was his real name and he was born in Ohio. He is a good citizen of the US. George Jones, William Anderson and Edward Murphy were clean. Alan Jackson was short, with black hair, moustache and a little beard and is now a guest of Hotel Lovin'Worthy. But we found five others to join our growing group of friends in the Kansas hotel. I know there are some terrorists hiding in the school systems, and I'm going to find them.

I gave the ones that turned out clean a little stipend for their inconvenience with my thanks, and asked for their help after explaining what we were doing with the terrorists. They all agreed to help in any way they could.

I had to call Mike back about the identity changer we had encountered back in Kansas City.

"Mike, don't you remember that guy we caught with a stolen car. We took his license and registration, and in his wallet was a card showing his name and address. His Social Security Number showed that it was issued in KC, but he spoke with a strong Pittsburgh accent, and he didn't know anything about KC."

"Yeah, so what?" He said.

"He had changed his identity, but forgot to learn to talk like the people where he was supposed to be living. We should have busted him. Sorry, my fault."

"I found a book that tells how to change your identity. There are specifics in it. Some of the main things are these, Drivers License, credit cards, utility bills, a library card, a wallet insert that you can put your fake name on, a monogram. But the two most important one are the Social Security Card and the Birth Certificate."

"This book has all the info in it for someone to do this."

I gave him the title of the book, the author, publisher and the place where I found it. He said that he would buy one just as soon as he could.

Chapter 4

Terrorist School

I stood up at the front of the conference room and began my little introduction.

"I have been elected by my Director and Lieutenant Lopez to have a few classes on terrorism. What a wonderful subject. This is the first, and I hope the last. This is the closest thing to a conference room we have here at the station, I hope everyone can get a seat. Let's begin with a few things I have found in the past".

"Those of us in law enforcement need to learn how to identify a terrorist. That means that we need to learn how to think like a terrorist. This is an extremely difficult task when you aren't accustomed to it."

"We're going to have to figure this out before they strike. We know a few things, but not enough. By the way, this is not a teacher-class exercise, this is audience participation, so if you have something, don't keep it to yourself."

"Normal people think one way. But evil people think in a completely different way. This is quite a quandary. The normal person wants to build up things and people. They help, they encourage, they love."

"The evil person wants to tear down and destroy people and things. They will burn down, kill, steal,

destroy, and if caught, they will laugh in your face
and lie about it or try to blame it on someone else,
usually someone they know who is blameless, in order to dirty their record if possible. These are all the
attributes of the devil. That is where all the evil in
this world comes from."

"There is no love in the evil person. Evil doesn't
smile or laugh, unless it's a fake laugh. You would do
well to look for the facial expression. That could be a
big help. They also do not help anyone, they are tak-
ers not givers. You might often hear words like this
from them." "I'll get you for that", or "What about
me?"

"Probably the biggest thing about the evil person
is this, they lie! They all think that the swearing in of
a witness in court with these words about truth is a
big joke."

"Raise your right hand. Do you swear that what
you are about to say is the truth, the whole truth and
nothing but the truth?"

"Of course, the answer must always be 'I do', but
do they really? Actually, they don't."

"This is a joke to them. Of course they will say
that it is the truth. It could have been just proven
false and testified to in open court two minutes ago,
and they would swear that it is the truth."

"The prosecutor asking the questions could say
of them, "We found this in your pocket" and they
would say "That isn't my pocket. Or that wasn't in
my pocket. Or where are the witnesses when you
found that? Or that isn't mine. Or no you didn't."

"Do you see what you are working against?"

"It is very hard to defend against this sort of thing, unless you know the truth and can prove it. Evil will help evil. It will stand together with them. Evil will lie to help another liar, then plot and plan how to discredit the one who is actually telling the truth."

"The normal person only needs to understand this, but never act on it. There is a fine line you must not cross. The evil will pull you down, and suck you in. You must brush it off!"

"The evil person will try to hire others to do the actual dirty work. That way, they think their hands are clean. Which, as we all know, is not true."

"There are many words that will help you find and describe the evil. Some of these words, they speak about others, some they attribute to themselves without even knowing it".

"The most common are liar, racist and hater. The evil person knows these words very well because they see them in the mirror every day. They seem to relish in it."

"A more inventive evil person will use some other words like these. Bad actor, calamity, clandestine, corrupt, depraved, double cross, false appearance of goodness, hypocrite, iniquity, mischief, misfortune, pernicious, perverted, pretender, surreptitious, vicious, venal, wicked. There are many more, if you want to use them."

"A word with more letters and syllables is always good for this kind of person. They feel superior if you are not familiar with the word and you might have to look it up."

"More importantly for you, most of these words can be easily attributed to the speaker of the words. So, if someone calls you a liar, it is likely that they are actually a liar because they are closer to it."

"But keep in mind that if you and your team or PD are working to ferret these criminals out, and someone on your team uses one of these words, they are not reflecting their own personal views."

"When he says, 'We have caught him in a lie several times before this.' What he is saying is a result of an investigation, it is not a reflection on him."

"Are there any questions?"

"Yes sir. I have a question that is bugging me and probably everyone else in the room." Ann Webster said.

"There must be character traits of these people that are evident to our sight. I have never even thought about trying to recognize this kind of person just by looking at them. Can you give us some clues or tell us where to find these things?" She said.

"Here we go on section two."

"Well Ann, it's a short list that I have, but I will give you everything I can. They are known as a manipulator. They want everything to be their way or the highway. A manipulator is someone who will change things for their own advantage. They will use personal influence, especially if it is unfairly done."

"The next thing you might notice is that they are nervous. They might look restless, uneasy or excited. They might have a twitch or act jerky. But one big thing is this. They know that everyone is less worthy for anything good than they are. The word worthy in their world means deserving. They feel that they are deserving of everything in the world and that they should not have to pay for any of it. It should be free to them and them only."

"The truth is, that they are not deserving of anything but jail or worse."

"One big problem with this whole scenario that I have given to you is that all this may come in phases. Today the person is sweet and kind, as kind as they can be, and tomorrow they are as ugly as a demon."

"Now, the person might be on drugs and if you could get them off of the drugs, then you would think the evil would leave them, but maybe not."

"These people enjoy seeing you or anyone hurt. They will belittle everyone they can. They will blame all of the world's ills or anyone they can. This is important too. The closer the problem is to them, the louder the blame is."

"Let me show you something on the board here. On the left side I will write 'evil'. We all know what that is. On the right side I will write 'good'. Again, we all know what that is. Now where do these two things come from? If I erase one of the letters 'O' from the word on the right, we have our answer. Now if I add a letter 'D' to the front of the word on the left, we have the other answer."

"Do we need to ask who we want to work for?"

I had to sit down, this is getting to me.

"Part three of this most interesting and illuminating class is weapons."

"A terrorist will almost always have a weapon of some kind. Guns are the first choice. Knives the second. One thing about the weapons, they are hard to hide in the summer because of the lack of clothing. You all know how to disarm an attacker with a knife and a gun. But a terrorist could have an explosive device with him or even strapped on him."

"Don't let yourself be drawn into this trap! If he has an IED in his hand or strapped on, and there is no one around within killing distance, just shoot him or the device. Blow him up! And hit the ground."

"But if there are people close to him, call the bomb squad immediately. Don't give him any chances to be stupid. Get all the people back as far as possible and try to distract him until the squad arrives."

"Oh, yes, I almost forgot. The Fifth Amendment is their friend. If there is the slightest chance that we might have them dead to rights, they will take the fifth to get out of it. It's too bad that there are so many lawyers in this country who enjoy getting the guilty ones free to do the same things again and again. But remember, Money rules the world. The lawyers want it too."

"I think they should be charged with Contempt of Court and Obstruction of Justice and held in jail until the questions are answered."

"Now if you want to go deeper into this, you could take some courses in psychology, maybe the library will have books available on the subject. I will try to find books on the subject and either buy the books or give you a list of the titles as soon as I can."

"Well folks, that's all I have right now. Lieutenant Lopez has given you all your assignments. Let's get out there and get rid of all the bad guys we can."

"One more thing. They pick schools because the students don't know enough to ask the right questions. The faculty doesn't seem to care because there is another teacher to pick up the load and the person doing the hiring only looks at the paperwork, not the whole person and their background."

Jim and I drew the south end of town from Fountain Boulevard down. This should be OK for us. There's not a lot of the kind of schools there that we are looking for in this area.

We have sixteen schools broken down into elementary, middle schools and high schools with one college. We'll start at the top with Pikes Peak College. The terrorists like the colleges best. If we find no one there maybe the rest will be clean.

Pikes Peak is a good school, but that's what they look for when they are trying to hide. It shouldn't take long after we interview a few students and the Dean for us to figure it out.

Jim and I explained to the Dean what we were doing and he said he would help in any way he could. He gave us a list of all the employees of the school and all the vendors he knew of. We forwarded it all to Lopez and his division.

Jim and I decided to walk around and try to look like we belonged there. When we could talk to a student, we gathered as much information as we could.

One female student looked uneasy when we talked to her. I took her name and pertinent info and tried to pry out the problem without seeming too nosy.

She indicated that this one teacher seemed like he was hitting on her. But she couldn't put her finger on it. I showed her a badge and said.

"Listen Alice, we will take care of this problem for you right now. You go on like nothing happened and don't talk to anyone about this until we get back to you."

We got his name and room number and went straight there.

The class was finished and the teacher was sitting at his desk at the front of the room.

"Good morning, sir. Are you Dennis Hubert?"

"Yes, I am. What can I do for you?" He said.

"We have an unusual bit of information we would like for you to confirm for us. Do you know a student named Alice, oh what's her name?" I asked.

"Oh, you mean Alice Foster. Yes, she is in one of my classes." He said.

His body language seemed normal. I peeked at Jim and he gave a nod.

"Do you know if she has a boy or girl friend?"

"There has been a boy talking to her during and after class from the beginning of this class. I thought he was a boyfriend because he was always touching her or hugging her. Let me see." He looked through the class register. "Here it is. His name is Roscoe Ryan." He said.

"Is he here in a class somewhere? We would like to speak to him."

He picked up his phone and called the administration office. In only a couple minutes he said. "He is in science class now. Room two fourteen."

Jim and I almost ran up the stairs to the room. Jim slipped into the room and told the teacher that we would like to speak to this student. Soon they were out in the hall with me.

"Roscoe, do you know a student named Alice Foster."

Suddenly he began to twitch and shake. Gotcha!

I had the handcuffs on him before he knew what was happening.

"What the hell! What are you doing?" He cried. He looked like he was going to sob all the way to the car. We took him and delivered him to a big muscular cop who takes these kind of cases and smooth's everything out, except maybe the perp.

Tomorrow we will find Alice and tell her what we have done. Maybe her nervousness and jitters will go away. We didn't get much done on our original plan today, but tomorrow is another day.

We found Alice and explained what we had done and all about Roscoe Ryan, the student who was causing her trouble.

"Every time that Roscoe was talking to me and begging for a date, Mr. Hubert was close by. I thought he was asking Roscoe to ask me. I really got that wrong. Please express my thanks to Mr. Hubert and tell him I'm sorry for the mix-up." She said.

We hung around Pikes Peak College for two more days, but nothing turned up. We finished the week in Widefield and Fountain. Back to the big city on Monday.

Chapter 5

We Get Calls

We get the strangest calls sometimes! I happened to be passing the dispatch office when I heard the phone ring. A woman politely answered with "911, what is your emergency?"

From the conversation, the person on the other end was calling to report a guy walking down the street with a bomb. I got my pen and when the dispatcher repeated the address, I wrote it down and ran up the stairs to get Jim.

Since I've driven to the Falcon airport many times I knew the way to the town and we were there in a matter of minutes.

I didn't get to hear the rest of the conversation. Maybe I should have waited. My phone was on and recorded it.

"I just called because he was going into the grocery store with it. He is still outside so you better get here quick! I could tell it was heavy because he was straining to lift it. I'm getting out of here." The caller said.

I sped toward the address I had and Jim asked a funny question.

"How would she know that it was a bomb?" He asked.

"It could be strapped to him, or he could be carrying it, or he could be yelling that he has a bomb. I don't know."

We drove to the address and saw a guy with a grocery cart with something big in it and he was headed toward the front door. I drove right up next to him and yelled at him to stop.

"What do you want?" He yelled back.

I jumped out of the car and went over to him.

"I had a call from a woman who said you had a bomb and were going to the grocery store. She thinks you're going to blow up the store."

"Me? I'm delivering some meat to the grocery store. Some guy parked his big ugly pickup in front of the dock where I unload. I couldn't get close enough to the store, so I have this cart and I'll have to take it into the store this way. There's my truck." He said and pointed to a big refrigerated local delivery truck.

Boy! Did that lady get it wrong!

"Wait, I'm going to help you and stop this parking problem both at the same time."

Jim and I helped him wheel his load of meat into the store. I walked up to the manager and explained what I wanted to do. He smiled a big smile and led me to the PA system.

"Attention, ladies and gentlemen! There is a large gray pickup truck parked at the loading dock of this store. We need to have it moved immediately. There are trucks with food to be delivered here waiting."

I saw some movement and a guy went outside to move his truck. What a surprise he'll get when Jim writes him a big ticket for blocking the dock and reprimands him harshly. I'll bet he won't do that again.

Once we got back outside I said to Jim. "I'm glad there wasn't a guy with a bomb here today."

The next day when Jim and I were visiting our favorite auto mechanic, Norm, we got a call on the radio that there was a report that a terrorist was found in a school in Goodland Kansas. I responded to the call with. "What do you want us to do about it? Goodland is easily two hundred miles away. That's almost four hours away and how would we find the guy anyway?"

"They said that someone has captured him and we were the closest big town that could handle him." She said.

Great! Let's drive tow hundred miles to a little town in Kansas in a car with a screaming siren and dodge every driver in the state. That sounds like so much fun. Jim stomped the gas pedal and we were off.

It wasn't hard to find the one guy in Goodland. It's a small town and everyone who had kids knew who this guy was. We turned him over to the local sheriff and called the FBI to come get him.

I took a few photos for our friends in Kansas and Missouri. They might know him.

Back at the Goodland Police Station while we waited for the FBI man, I was questioning one of the other terrorists that we caught. He was very full of himself. He was a drama queen and liked to boast about how smart he was and how we were so stupid to have such a society without their kind of law. I decided I would be the 'nice cop' for him.

"Are there teachers on other roads in Kansas or in other states."

"Of course. We have people in every town on I-70 from Kansas City to Goodland."

Ted and Mike are going to have their hands full. Just listing the towns on I-70 is a daunting task. The bigger ones are KC, Lawrence, Topeka, Junction City, Manhattan, Abilene, Salina, Russell, WaKeeney, Hays, Oakley, Colby and Goodland.

I called Ted and relayed the news to him.

"We have a gigantic problem! Call Mike and all the people you can. We must get this cleaned up! Since we are in Goodland now, we will try to find the ones here and remove them."

While he was going on with his blowhard noise, he made a very chilling statement to me. It turned me from nice cop to bad cop.

"We have teachers in every town on I-70 from Kansas City to Goodland. They won't be noticed there. The Americans are too stupid to see them, because we are way smarter than you." Mr. Terrorist said.

I'll bet that if they are stationed in Kansas on I-70, they are also stationed in other states like Missouri and Colorado along I-70. We've got a big problem.

He began to preach to me using big words. He was trying to prove that he was smarter than me and that he could prove it. I must admit he used some fifty cent words, and was very impressive in that regard, but the context of his whole speech was crap. And that was the first word that I started with.

"Your whole story is – wait let me use a big word just for you – CRAP! I know a lot of descriptive words that apply to you and your mission. Let's start with four letters. Crap, evil, liar, mean, fool, shit. Now let's move on to five letters, racist, hater, blame, clown. I've got some really good words to describe you and your movement. Let's try a few."

"Greedy, amateur, malcontent, malignant, malicious, gain, bushel, loss, commit. Wasn't that fun? I just told you a story of the rest of your life. It starts with your lust for power and greed. You gained a bushel of loss. And it ends with you being committed to a wonderful place like Leavenworth or MAX for the rest of your miserable life."

I was so glad to turn this clown over to someone who would escort him to a maximum security facility and kiss him goodbye. I wanted to shoot him, but the FBI man got there before I could.

Jim and I stopped in Simla and Calhan and picked up two easy-to-find ones for our growing group of crazies. I'm going to enjoy this question and answer session. If this is all true, we're going to need more personnel to help with the load.

We know that only one guy fixed it so more could come in. I have a feeling that there is someone somehow connected to the Kansas school system or the Legislature. There's a lot of work to do in Kansas. That should keep the guys busy.

Another call we got was from a woman who said that she saw a tornado on the northwest side of the Springs from her house. There were three things wrong with her story. We don't get tornados here. From the address that she gave the 911 operator, she couldn't have seen the tornado if there was one. And it was not the time of year when tornados form in any part of this country.

But we sent a Highway Patrol Officer out to check it out. He reported back that it was a beautiful day with bright sun, minimal wind and no rain. It was a false report. Big surprise!

I hope she got some satisfaction out of the call she made which was a lie.

While Jim and I were out east in the boondocks, there were a few 911 calls that Lopez told us about later. During the telling, he was smiling most of the time. I never did see any reason for a smile about a call like that. I always thought they were serious.

"We have been getting 911 calls every few days that would have no voice or maybe static when the dispatcher answered. While you guys were out messing around in the countryside another one of them came in and the dispatcher found an address by crossing it with another call in the area."

"I sent a car to the address but there was no one home. Now we know there is a mysterious problem. I called the phone company to come out and help us."

"One of their men climbed the poles around the two houses there. He found that squirrels had been eating the insulation from the wires and they would touch when the wind blew a tree branch into the pole. The people who live in one of the houses came home while we were there. They told us that there have been a lot of squirrels around the area and they get into their houses as well."

"I called animal control and insisted they come out right away. They were not happy! Now they have the task of moving the squirrels to another location, covering all the phone lines so this won't happen again and finding a way to keep them from invading other poles and people's houses"

"I'm loving it." Lopez said.

Chapter 6

Local Schools

Lopez decided to assign all of our team an area of town and we would go to each school and interview the Principals and teachers and when we could, students. We were to ask about the possibility of crazy teachers or other employees working there.

Everyone went thru the schools assigned to them. We caught a few questionable teachers and students, but not many. I called for a car to pick up the ones we found and take them to the office. While we were close to the shop, Jim and I decided to go see our old friend Norm.

"Hey, guys! What's new in the world of crime and criminals?" Norm said.

"We've got our fishing poles out and we are casting everywhere we can." Jim said. "Only a few nibbles."

"DJ, we've been building these cars and trucks for everyone else for years now, and you have never said what car would turn your crank. What would you like to have?" Norm asked.

"Ya know, Norm. In all of the lists of old cars and trucks there are out there, the only one I would like to have the most, is a 1940 Ford Woody Wagon."

"I wish I could sing and dance too." Jim said. "But I can't and never will."

They both stood there and laughed until it got to be embarrassing.

Norm and Jim laughed for the rest of the day about that. You can't talk to people when they get like that.

Everybody on the team was out in their areas investigating teachers and anyone that worked in the school system. At a couple of the schools, we found a few students who wanted to talk about their bad teachers and a few teachers that wanted to talk about their bad students. Most of it was just complaining. It began to sound like a political rally.

After a couple of hours of this we gave up and went back to the station and had some very strong black coffee and a lot of silence.

At least one of the Officers from our PD has visited every school in the Pikes Peak district. Collectively, we found only a few of the unhinged people that we were hunting. I feel good about that. From all the research that we have done, most of the problem has been centered in the far east and west parts of the country. And for some strange reason, the Kansas City area. Jim and I may have to go back to Kansas City for a while to help with their problem.

Jim and Lopez have been on the background checks of Downey ever since we got back from DC. They checked every name of anyone he had contact with during his tenure in the State Government. We had ten people on the job, but we still have a long list of names. About a quarter of them have been checked out and only two have showed up on the wrong side so far. Those two have been incarcerated in the cross-bar hotel.

As the DC people go to the Kansas and Missouri capitals there might be others. There must be others that we can find. We'll start in the State Capitals and ask questions. We have alerted all the law enforcement in the two cities to be on the look-out for them.

"Did the Congressman and other two have people that they met with regularly?"

"I'm sure they did. We're checking all the people in DC, Topeka and Jefferson City. Maybe we'll get some names." Lopez said.

"We need to divide up and run down the leads. Maybe we should examine each one and learn what we can do to recognize them and stop them before they do something terrible." Jim said.

Sergeant Solano spoke up and began to tell what he found out about the one of the professors.

"One of Lopez's girls, Officer Bonita Hernandez, found a professor who found and corrupted a teacher and another professor to give a job to one of his friend's students. It turned out to be Downey. The Campus Police will pick up the professor as soon as they can locate him. He seems to have disappeared."

"It turned out that the teacher was innocent. She was only trying to help another teacher who asked a favor. She didn't know his motives. The professor is the guilty one, and we will put him away for good." Sergeant Solano said.

"But let me tell you what the real bonanza was that we found. We found several boxes of papers and notebooks in the bottom of a locker hidden in the back of a room in the basement. They look like they are notes taken during classes. There are names here and there of students and one name indicating a Professor Johnson."

"This professor taught Math, and Science, but especially Astronomy. We haven't found the professor or the students named there as yet. We don't know the dates that the notes were taken and we don't know how long all the paperwork was stored in the lockers."

"The title on one of the notebooks is 'Astrophysics'. It wasn't bad enough that this guy was infecting the classes in Math and Science, but these others too."

"It said in the notebook that the professor taught Astronomy just like he did all the other subjects. He would say that there is no God and went on to talk about how God couldn't do certain things that men obviously can't do either."

"It was hard for the students to debate this because he would ask, "Could you do this?" Obviously the answer was always no. Any reasonable person knows that they can not do what God can do."

"Then he would come back with, 'What did I just tell you?'"

"If someone would talk about Jesus, he would blow it off as hearsay."

"In Astronomy he taught, more like he preached, that 'there is no God' to all those who would listen and some that wouldn't. Many of the students have walked out of his classes and dropped him as a teacher. There have been many complaints about him, but the administration has kept him on."

"I have a handwritten note here that reads like satan himself wrote it. Probably in this professor's handwriting. Here it is."

"There is no way that one person, or god, could put all those stars out there or make a big world like this. He wrote. Notice that God is spelled with a small G."

"In the notebook, it shows where students asked questions like this. 'But that's what it says in the Bible. Then how did they all get there?' A student asked."

"It was all the accidental explosions after the Big Bang." He said.

"What about the moon? Where did it come from?" A different student asked.

"That was just another accident when the moon crashed into the world and part of it stayed close and now it orbits around the world. This all happened billions of years before people were on the earth." He said.

"This is all the words of a supposedly brilliant and informed professor of Astronomy. He should have been let go years ago."

"This professor doesn't go to church, or a mosque, or anything. He would always say that he had to study and he was too busy to go to church when asked. Actually, he doesn't believe in God, or any god, so he doesn't go to church at all. He repeats that he doesn't believe in anything over and over." Sergeant Solano ended his brief and sat down.

I know that I have a special visit with the administration coming up very soon. Jim and I will enjoy this one a lot.

Jim and I sat down with the Dean and some of the faculty during the visit to ask questions. They admitted that there were many complaints about this teacher.

"Why didn't you fire him?"

"He has tenure due to the length of time he taught here." The Dean said.

"Did you give him a warning?"

"Yes. More than one, but he didn't seem to hear or understand me at the time." He said.

"Where is he now? Dou you have his name, address, or phone number? Do you have a forwarding address?"

"We don't know where he went or when he left. His room was cleaned out and his computer was erased of all personal information." He said.

"How could you not have any info on this man?"

"We found that he got into the office here and removed all files with his name on them. It's like he was never here." He said.

It's hard for me to understand how our people do these things. I thought the schools have a handle on everything they did, but now this.

I have a pile of notes and notebooks that I need to go through. I've got to get back to the station or my den and study this stuff. There is a lot and I don't want to burden the others with this.

It took a few days, but what I found was right along the same line of our original ideas. I need to brief Lopez and the others on this stuff as soon as I can.

The next day I took the time to explain what we found on Downey to Lopez and the team.

"When the Colorado Governors Assistant got sick and was in failing health they went looking for a replacement. I still wonder about that. He was in good shape when I knew him and it seemed to me that he got sick all of a sudden. I wonder if he didn't have some outside help."

"Guess who I think might be responsible for all of it? The third guy, Downey, got hired into the Governor's Inner Circle right then. I've got most of the background on Downey. Here it is."

"You must have a High School Diploma or a GED in order to get a job as a Law Clerk. Downey took the GED and passed it about two or three months after he appeared in Denver. He worked as a Law Clerk for two years and took night and on-line classes to get the required Associate Degree."

"He then advanced to a job as a Paralegal. Now he needed to get his Bachelors Degree. This took two more years of both night and on-line classes again."

"Now came the hard part for Downey. To become a lawyer, he needed before entering the Law School, to take the LSAT, or Law School Admission Test and pass it. Then he must get a three year degree in Law. It must be done at the college and it must be done not faster or slower than the required time. This means that he was away from his job and in classes for a period of thirty six months."

"That would normally have taken him out of circulation from his professor friend and all the others. But we found his footprints and fingerprints all over the State political arena. He was doing all this at CU in Boulder, so he was not far away. I imagine that he was in daily contact with the others."

"Once all this is done, the Bar Exam is looming in the background, and you go nowhere without it. After this comes the title Juris Doctor with the appropriate letters after your name, (JD)."

"What this tells me is that they will spend many years developing their plan before they actually put it into motion. That in itself is scary, but we will find a way to stop them!"

"I found one batch of notebooks with Downey's name on them that seem to have all the courses that he took during the college years. I checked with the school and this is their required class list for their law degree."

"It takes a hundred and twenty four credits to graduate from the Political Science courses. There are ninety five hours of the law courses. Difficult courses! That means that there are about thirty hours of Math and English and speech and writing and all that other stuff. These guys have to be dedicated to hating us to go through all this just so they can find a way to kill us."

The name on the notebook. Was it a student? Was it a teacher? Was it the professor? Was it a spy? We don't know anything! I hope there are some latent fingerprints on it. I put it in a plastic bag to take to the lab.

Chapter 7

Psychopath

It was a good move to come back to our hometown and get to renew old acquaintances and relatives.

When the Director told me that we were going to be hunting for terrorists and our usual brand of crooks, I tried to find out what drives a terrorist.

It came to me at a time when I was not trying so hard to remember certain things. I have known a friend from years back who went into medicine. Maybe he will be able to help. I just have to find him.

It took me a few days to locate Doctor Louis Whitman. I called him and made an appointment.

"DJ! It's been a long time since I have heard from you. What are you doing now? Tell me all about your life and times." Lou said.

"Hi Lou. I am working for the Government. I've been doing this for quite a long time. My family and I have recently returned to our home here in the Springs. I have an office downtown in the Police Station."

"You're a cop?" He said.

"Well, kind-of." I opened my coat for him to see James Bond and showed him my badge.

"Wow! I never would have guessed!" He said.

"You must never tell anyone about what you just saw." I pointed to the gun and badge.

"OK, I've already forgotten it. What is it you came to see me about? It must be important for a person with that badge to be in my little office." He said.

"You certainly have heard and seen all the attacks by what they are calling terrorists. We have been alerted that there are a group of these people here in the Springs. I need help to identify these people before they do something terrible. Maybe there is a psychological trait that we can see. We need help!"

"I think I can give you a place to start. These people are called Psychopaths. Many years ago a doctor named Robert Hare devised a list of possible and probable traits of a psychopath. It's called a psychopathy checklist. It has been studied and revised, but it is clear what to look for." He said.

"Is this something that we will need a doctor to tell us what we found?"

"No, no. There are twenty items on the list and they are named so that anyone, even you, can understand what to look for." Lou said with a big smile.

He went to his bookshelves and pulled out one well used hardback and opened it.

"I will make you a copy of the list directly out of the book." He said.

He held the book over the copier and ran the pages off.

"There must be fifteen pages or more here."

"The list is on the first page and the explanations of each item follow. You will need the explanations to help you understand what it is." He said.

I looked at the first page to see if I had a chance with this level of craziness. It read like this.

1. Superficial Charm
2. Grandiose Sense of Self-Worth
3. Need for Stimulation
4. Pathological Lying
5. Manipulation
6. Lack of Guilt
7. Shallow Effect
8. Lack of Empathy
9. Parasitic Lifestyle
10. Poor Behavior
11. Promiscuous
12. Early Behavior Problems
13. Lack of Realistic Goals
14. Impulsivity
15. Irresponsibility
16. Failure to Accept Responsibility
17. Many Short Term Relationships
18. Juvenile Delinquency
19. Revocation of Conditional Release
20. Criminal Versatility

"Wow! Big List! I've been told that I have some of these things. I'm not proud to say that though."

"This list is a guide. If you are interviewing a person who you think is a terrorist, it would be good to look for these items. If there are only one or two, that could be quite normal. Especially if they are scared that they could be arrested for a crime they did not commit." He said.

"What you are looking for is the overall score that these item adds up to in your mind. The higher the score they register with you, the more chance that you have found one. These are the people who you need to watch for more information." Lou said.

"Most of this I can figure out or I have already seen before. But what is number nineteen?"

"Repeated failure by the terrorist to turn his life around when he has a chance to redeem himself. The threat of being punished does not contain a problem to him. Jail and parole mean nothing to him."

"Keep in mind, that this list does not only apply to terrorists, but to the general population. Thieves, traitors, terrorists, murderers, every kind of criminal that you can think will exhibit some, if not most, of these traits." He said.

"Oh, you're a lot of fun! I could have gone to a horror movie and had more fun than this."

Lou enjoyed my comment and laughed a lot about it.

I thanked Lou for his help and told him. "I feel sure we will need a lot more of your help. I hope you will be available."

"Just call. I'll make time for you." He said.

I took the paperwork to the station and showed it to Lopez. He called one of the computer savvy officers over and told her to make copies for each person and we will go over it all together.

We spent an hour brainstorming the list that Lou gave me. I am beginning to understand a little more of it now. I'm going to need a lot more help from Dr. Lou.

Lopez got his people on it right away. They made a little pamphlet of the items on the list. They made lists to be posted on the walls next to our desks in every office.

I put one on a slide out drawer in the interrogation room where I could look at it as I was talking to these people. Some of them are more off the track than others, and I want to be ready.

Chapter 8

Lets go Camping

Jim and I had been out all day searching every nook and cranny for the bad guys. We found one, but he was just a little drug dealer and didn't count much on our scorecard.

About a half an hour after we reported to Lopez and got our coffee, Jim and I were just talking and I said. "I heard that there is a camp up in the mountains where some of these terrorists hide out. I wish I knew where it was."

A voice from across the room rang out. "I do!" She said.

Officer Julie Cavalli hurried to my desk and sat down.

"I think I have some news that will make you wake up and dance a jig, DJ." She said.

"Great! Let's have it!"

"My friend Jane and I were out walking in the forest looking for evidence of deer last weekend. We'll be hunting in a few months and we want to know where they hang out. We came upon this camp. There were about twenty guys there. We saw several guns and knives, but no explosives. I don't know who they are, but they aren't in a regular place for camping."

"We can show you where it is. She isn't a cop. She's a tour guide and she knows every nook and cranny

in these woods. She carries a gun but not like we do."
She said.

We went to Lopez and she explained all that she
had told Jim and I.

"Good! Let's go in the morning about seven am".
Lopez said. She was right, that made me very happy
and excited.

"Attention! We will be going up to an area in the
mountains tomorrow. We will leave here about seven
in the morning. Bullet proof vest and weapons are
the uniform of the day. No uniforms! Dirty and
ripped clothes that look like we are hunters are the
best thing to wear. That's all. See you at seven." Lopez said.

I put on my best dirty, torn and ripped old work
clothes that I could find. Next comes the vest and, of
course, I can't go without James Bond.

Julie and Jane led us to the exact spot where the
camp was. The residents were just sitting around
smoking and drinking. I don't think they heard us
until we were right on top of them.

We surrounded the camp and came in slow. We
crept up to about half of them before someone saw
us. Three of them jumped up and pulled their guns.
Just as one was pointing at me I fired.

"Physstt!"

Two more jumped up with guns in hand and Jim
and Lopez took care of them.

"Physstt"! "Bang!"

The rest of them decided it wasn't a good idea to try it. We collected all the weapons and handcuffed them all and began the long trek down to level ground. More level ground that is.

Just as we were passing along a steep drop into a canyon, three of them broke to the left and began to run toward the cliff. They continued to run as fast as they could right off the trail and fell the hundred feet to the bottom. Still in handcuffs. I don't get it! Did they know that there was a cliff there or were they just trying to get away?

We stopped and assessed our possibilities of getting the three bodies out without more injury or death to us or the prisoners. We decided that we would send someone up for them. It's far too dangerous with all the baggage that we have.

I took my place in the back of the parade with James Bond in my hand and we continued down the hills to our vehicles. The kid in the back began to talk to me and he had a very unusual story to tell.

"I saw an ad on the internet for kids to go to a big party in the Rockies, and since I already lived here I went. But there's something bad wrong here. All these guys talk about is killing people."

"Who are you kid? What's your name and where were you born?"

"My name is Andrew Woods. I was born in Dormont, Pennsylvania. It's a town in the Pittsburgh district. My folks moved here when my dad was transferred to Fort Carson." He said.

"Give me a brief rundown on you."

"I can only tell you what they told me. After high school, my dad worked his way through college at Pitt. He got his degree in Business, but there weren't any jobs available so he joined the Army. After basic and OCS, he was a Second Lieutenant and was sent to Fort Polk. Mom and I were going to move there, but Dad called and told her not to come until he got his next assignment."

"We all moved to Fort Sill in two years, then to Fort Hood and now to Fort Carson. Dad and Mom live here in town on East Bijou just past Circle. I hope we can stay here. I like it here and I have a good job. Dad's a Major now. I hope he goes all the way." Andy said.

"What do you do?"

"I went into Real Estate. I got my license after high school when I found a sales job open. I didn't like sales very much, so I got into the appraisal side of the business. I liked that but an opening in Property Management came open and they selected me." He said.

"Let me check all this out and I'll call you. I think I can use you on our team. Do you know how to handle a pistol or rifle?"

"A little but I would need a lot of help." He said.

"If I offered you a job with us, would you want it?"

"Yes! I think I would like to get rid of those creeps like the ones you guys just caught." He said.

"What makes you say that?"

"They hate all people who believe in God. These guys are nuts. All they talk about are all the kinds of different ways that they know to kill people. They're all wrong. One guy said that Allah commanded him to kill anyone who did not believe what he believes. I don't want to be anywhere near them." He said.

The trip back to the station was unusual. I had to threaten them several times to stop the yelling and swearing. Finally I stopped the truck and said that I would stand them outside and shoot them one by one if there wasn't quiet. That shut them up!

Once we returned to the city and began to get back to normal, I took Andy to a private room where we could talk without being interrupted.

"Look, if you check out on my background and you want to work with us. You will have to go to school for at least a year. I can set up the courses for you and you could do them on-line and at nights. But the courses are difficult. I'll give you a list of them and then you can decide.

"You could work at your regular job until you finished the courses, then we could bring you on here."

"That sounds good to me. When can I start?" He asked.

"I'll work on it right away and call you with dates and times."

"Were you in the Service? You sound like you know a lot about the military." He asked.

"Yes. I did my time and a little more."

"What did you do?" He asked.

"I was in – uh – logistics."

"What's that?" He asked.

"It's – uh – servicing the Army in the field."

"Did you get a lot of medals? My dad doesn't have very many." He said.

"Yeah. I have a whole rainbow of them. But that's enough about me. Let's get back to you."

"I will get a list of the courses that you will have to take and pass in the first semester of this course. I would like for you to tell me then if you want to go on with these studies."

"The first group are Criminal Justice courses and they are absolutely necessary. There are only thirty eight credits, but you will need them in order to go on."

I handed him a paper with all the courses listed on it.

LAW 100	Introduction to Criminal Justice	3
LAW 110	Introduction to Juvenile Justice	3
LAW 130	Modern Police Procedures	3
LAW 190	Criminal Investigation	3
LAW 200	Penology and Corrections	3
LAW 260	Criminal Law	3
LAW 275	Police Photography	2
LAW 283	Legal Studies	2
LAW 320	Criminal Evidence	3
LAW 405	Research Methods	3

"This is the second group. Only nine credits but as before, you will need them."

I gave him the second sheet of courses.

LAT 101	Introduction to Law	3
LAT 220	Legal Research	3
LAT 230	Real Property	3

"You'll also need some background in Politics."
Then the third sheet of courses.

PSC 101	American National Government	3
PSC 111	Understanding the State Constitution	1
PSC 320	Public Administration	3
PSC 375	Seminar on Terrorism	3

"And no one gets away without Math and English."

By the time I gave him this last sheet, he was beginning to wear down.

Math	3
English	3
Ethics	3
History	3
Writing	3

"You will have seventy two credits and you will be more than halfway toward your degree. You will also have enough for me to hire you and continue with your training and on-the-job training."

"I hope I can do this. This looks like something I could enjoy for many years." He said.

Chapter 9

Salt Lake City

It was Wednesday the first of June when the Director called Jim and I into his office.

"Good morning DJ and Jim, I have a job for you two. You aren't going to like it, but I don't have anyone with the qualifications to complete this one but you. You are the best that I have for this job, so you are elected. Have a seat."

The Director was having a good time explaining our next assignment. Maybe too much fun. He was wearing an ear to ear smile the whole time he was talking.

"The Director in Salt Lake City called for some help. He thinks there is a counterfeit ring working there. They have found hundreds of instances of counterfeit money in and around the city in the last few months."

"You have a past record of finding and stopping counterfeiters, so I am assigning you this project. I have made a contact at the university there for you. Both of you.

"Also he said that he would like us to teach some classes at the University on how to recognize counterfeit money and what to do about it." The Director said.

"I know you have done classes for the team in Kansas City and Colorado Springs. Since you two have done this before, I agreed that you would be glad to help."

"DJ, you will be a professor at the University of Utah. They have a faculty position waiting for you. They will provide everything you need including the necessary books. You must tell them the name of the books that you want, and they will supply them."

I was taking notes when he began the talk. That last one surprised me.

"Jim would be a student and only be in your last class of the day. That way you could walk out together and DJ would give Jim a ride. This is all for appearances. No one will be the wiser."

"This is important." The Director said. "I need to know what name you are going to use there. I know you can't or won't use DJ."

"Let's make one up right now then. I like the first initial D, what about David? David was after God's heart and I am too."

"OK. Now the last name." He said.

"Wynn!" Jim said. "We are winners, after all."

"I love it!" The Director said. "It's nice to meet you, David Wynn, I would like you to meet your partner, Jim McCoy."

Jim played along. "Hello, Mister Wynn, I'm glad to meet you too."

We all shook hands like we were first meeting each other. We stood there like fools and laughed about it for several minutes.

Before I go to Salt Lake City I need some information. I could call someone there, but I don't know anyone. I did once, but the phone number is no good now. I talked to the Director and he talked to the one out there, but they didn't have the answers that I wanted. We do have the dates and times but that's all.

I've been to Salt Lake a few times before, but I wanted to do more research on the whole area this time. It's different now. Those first times were mostly fun and games with the WRAT team. I put in for a job there, but didn't get it. I offered marriage, but didn't get it. Maybe this time I'll succeed at something.

I put my background research hat on and went to work. I spent two days in the libraries around town. I don't have any of the information that I need at home. But after an intense program in the main library downtown, I found what I wanted.

Salt Lake City was founded by the Mormons in 1847. Fort Douglas, named for Steven Douglas, a famous speaker in that time, was built on the hill on the north east side in 1861. President Lincoln authorized the construction of it. Fort Douglas houses US Army artillery units and their supporting units.

There is a monument made of steel in the middle of town built to honor the California Sea Gulls that came all the way from the Pacific coast and devoured the crickets that were destroying the Mormon's crops in 1848. The birds saved the crops that saved the people and their town.

The Temple was begun in 1853 and after forty years was completed in 1893. The State Capitol was completed in 1915. Both buildings only a few blocks apart.

There is a branch of the Federal Reserve Bank of San Francisco located there. The city also serves as a smelting center for the minerals mined in the region. These minerals are gold, silver, copper and lead. There is a gigantic open pit copper mine there.

I didn't know there was so much to learn about the city and the state. Now that I have learned all about the city, it's time for me to get back to work.

"You will teach Economics, Finance and Accounting, Banking or anything that you can think of about money. You are, of course, the only expert that we know around here. You will have full control of the course."

The Director told Jim and I to go to Salt Lake City and report in at the University of Utah. The Director would make up our life stories for us and Jim would be a student and I would be fully qualified as an instructor.

"I will need to have someone in the local PD as my personal contact like I have here with Lieutenant Lopez."

"Yes. I have already taken care of that. That person will be Lieutenant Raymond Wright." He said. "This is all his information and phone numbers."

He handed me a sheet with all the info on it. When we got out of the Director's office, I called Ted.

I explained to Ted what the assignment was and why we would need the plane. We set a date for him to fly out. He will return home on a commercial flight from Peterson Field after we feed him a good meal and let him sleep the night in a warm bed.

I was sitting in the office at Falcon Airport when that beautiful blue plane touched down on the runway. I always liked the name Beechcraft. It sounds good to me.

"Hi Ted. Was it a good flight?"

"Yes. I really like our big blue plane. What's going on that you needed it here?" Ted asked.

"Jim and I have an assignment in Salt Lake with an undisclosed time on it. We could be there for a few months, probably more. Of all things, it has to do with counterfeiting again. But I get the high class job. The Director has made me a Professor of Finance, and I'll be teaching a class at the University of Utah."

"So after all these years, you finally had someone say that they thought you are smart." Ted said and laughed.

I did chuckle a little at that one.

"Jim is going as my nephew, my brother's son."

"But you don't have a brother." Ted said.

"I know that, but they don't."

"He will be a student in my class. In addition, Jim and I would be staying together in Salt Lake City and looking for terrorists. We will be adhering to the schedule of the school. When school was out we will be free to go anywhere in the area or go home if we wanted to do so."

We decided to fly the blue plane to the Salt Lake airport and take a taxi to town. I bought a paper and we sat in a restaurant and searched the automotive ads for a car. I found a '62 Pontiac in one of the ads. The ad said it ran good, the price was right and when I called, he said he would drive to the restaurant for us to see it.

He arrived just after we had finished our lunch and we all went for a little ride. It has had some body work done and is now three colors, but it is solid and all the rust was removed.

"I like it." Jim said.

"I do too. How much is it?"

"If you want it right now, I would take four hundred." He said.

"Does that include a clear title and plates?"

"Sure." He said.

"Let's go!"

We drove to the DMV and got the title and the plates changed and took our seller home. Then back to the restaurant to find a motel and a map.

I had made reservations at the Rodeway Inn, and luckily I had an address for it. It took a little time for us to get our bearings, but I found the motel and we got checked in.

"Good morning class. My name is David Wynn. These classes are Money and Banking. And I am your instructor for the next semester or two."

"Before we start, I have three rules for the conduct of this class. They are hard and fast rules. Here they are."

"There will be no photos of the instructor or any member of the class taken at any time by any person! Any person taking a photo described will have the camera confiscated, they will fail the class and be escorted to jail for questioning."

"There will be no variance of these rules. If you cannot obey them, leave now! But leave the camera phone when you do."

"Why are the rules so harsh?" One student asked.

"We are dealing with terrorists in this country. We don't know is and who isn't. I will be talking about money and all the trimmings. Terrorists want to kill us, but they want all of our money also."

"What they really want is for all of us to lay down and die so they can walk in and take everything we have. We, however, are not willing to do this."

"I have counted. There are twenty one of you. If you want to stay, bring your phone or camera up here and put it in this box. I will have it cleaned and returned by the end of the day."

All but one brought their phone up to the desk.

"What about you?" I asked and pointed to the boy.

"You can't have my phone!" He said with a smile. "I'll fight you for it!"

"Really?"

I pulled out James Bond for him to see and Jim removed his phone. I called the Campus security number they gave me and a big burly cop came to the room.

"What can I do for you sir?" He said.

"This kid wanted to fight me for his phone. He must have some very interesting numbers on it.

Would you deliver him to the local Police and have them examine his phone very carefully. Tell them David Wynn sent him there."

The Campus cop took him away in handcuffs. The kid wasn't smiling anymore.

The rest of the class looked shocked but there were smiles beginning on most of their faces.

"Well guys, let's get started. There will be several subsections to this course. The first part is counterfeiting."

"To counterfeit means to make an imitation of an original with a view to defraud. To forge, to make an imposter or a sham. So you see what we are dealing with. Counterfeiting is a whole different ballgame than Accounting and Banking."

Before we started, I handed out latex gloves so they would not get fingerprints on anything I might need.

"Who would like to pass out these books for me?"

"I will." A student named Mike said. I like him already.

I handed Mike the books we had talked about and he passed them out to the class.

"We'll go through the book chapter by chapter. If you want to read ahead go ahead. But I will continue at my own pace. This is important stuff."

"The bell is going to ring any second, so I will see you all tomorrow." And the bell rang just in time.

Since I have a lot more time between discussions, I can explain more and more about what I want them all to do to help find the counterfeiters. They don't know that they will be helping yet, but I will work into it slowly.

"If you are in a bank receiving money from the public, you need to know if and when you are handed a piece of funny money. I can tell you that it is not funny."

"You all have some paper money with you. I put a magnifying glass there on your desks for each of you. Pull out a few of your bills and we'll go over a few of the little niceties the Treasury has done."

"The US Government prints our paper money with a lot of, let's call them deterrents, in them. Many little things that are nearly impossible to copy by a novice, or a computer."

"Real money is printed five times. The first color is green and then black. After that they tint the paper. Next red and blue fibers are inserted into each bill. There is also a watermark. Lastly there is a cloth strip."

"Two of the most obvious deterrents to counterfeiting are the large portrait and the watermark. The watermark and the portrait are always of the same person."

"The watermark is located on the right hand side near the serial number and these are vital in authenticity."

"Take your magnifying glass and examine your bills to find what I have told you."

"Counterfeiters don't bother with ones and five dollar bills. But you can always use them to look for the things we have talked about. They can help you to see those details."

"The counterfeit portrait is lifeless and flat to the naked eye, so you must look closely."

"Notice the fine line printing behind the portrait on the front side of the real bill, and behind the building on the back. Use the magnifying glass."

"Yes, I see the lines. Boy, are they ever small!" Josh said.

"I don't see any lines." A voice said from the back of the classroom.

"Let me have a look at that."

Adam brought his twenty dollar bill and his magnifying glass up to my desk. I took the glass and carefully inspected the bill.

"Well ladies and gentlemen, we have a winner. Adam has the first fake in the house, a brand new twenty dollar bill. Let me put that in an evidence bag. There might be some fingerprints on the bill. And besides that, you don't want to go to jail for passing bad money."

"Adam, we'd better get a look at the rest of your money. I hope there's no more of this kind of thing." I said.

Adam emptied his pockets and we all picked up magnifying glasses and began to search for clues.

"The counterfeit usually has details that merge into the background which makes them too dark to detect. I think this is the only one you have." I said.

"Where did you get this bill?"

"I got this at the bank down on Fifteenth South."

"We need to take a little trip." I said to Jim.

"Class dismissed. See you all tomorrow."

When school was out, Jim and I took a ride to the bank Adam told us about. I put on a disguise on the way there. We walked in a few minutes before closing and asked for the bank president. He came out to the lobby and I said.

"I have a counterfeit bill I would like to run through your C machine. Would that be alright with you?"

"Who are you and why are you asking such a question?" He asked.

"Let's go to your office and we will explain."

I showed him my badge and told him why we wanted to see the machine.

"If this bill does not register then your machine is faulty and we will need to get you another machine and check all the money in the vault."

"I can't let you do that." He said.

"Well then, I will shut down this bank and arrest you and all the people who work here. You decide."

He gave me the same look that those guys we pick up on the street give me. I have to shoot them in the thigh to get them to talk. Our bank President is coming very close to that.

I took out my phone and called the Director.

"Good afternoon sir. This is David Wynn. Would you please send a few agents over to the bank on Fifteenth South. I have a group of people who would like to live with us for a few days or maybe longer. I will need another counterfeit detection machine and a special ride for the Bank President also." - - - "There are about a dozen or so." - - "Yes, thank you."

"Your ride will be right here." I told the President.

Mister Bank President slowly sank down into his chair with a dejected look and just stared out into space. I've seen that look before.

Jim closed and locked the front doors and stood guard there till our backup arrived.

When the USSS agents brought the machine, the agents took it into the vault and began examining ever bill they could find. It registered that about half of what they picked out is counterfeit. The FBI agent took Mr. Flynn into custody and ushered him back to their office for questioning. I would like to have been there. But sometimes you can't have everything.

Once we were done with the president, I took a good twenty from the vault to be returned to Adam tomorrow.

The next day in class I announced that we would be going out on field trips to the city and examining how money works there.

"We will be broken up into teams of two. Each team will be assigned a block and they are to scrutinize each business for good and bad practices. Write things down. Take pictures or video."

"THERE WILL NOT BE ANYTHING POSTED TO THE INTERNET. ANYONE WHO DOES THAT WILL FAIL THE CLASS AND SPEND TIME IN JAIL! I will personally escort them to the jail. They know me down there."

"Don't forget what I said. You know what I can do."

"The photos and video will only be used here in class and then completely erased for the next adventure!"

We spent nearly a month out on the town and found a lot more counterfeit than I expected. After all the classes and hands-on that this class has had, I thought I would try to trick them.

I still have that special roll-top desk I bought for my wife many years ago. And in one of the special little drawers was still an envelope with the Sawbuck ten dollar bill and the original. Inside were two clear evidence envelopes marked A and B. Inside each envelope is one crisp ten dollar bill. I brought them with me especially for this purpose. Let's see if any of them can tell the difference.

Chapter 10

Return To School

I displayed the bills to the class the next day.

"Look at these two ten dollar bills and tell me if one or both are real or not, and which one and your reason for the choice. Do not take them out of the clear envelopes. Use the latex gloves that you have in your desk."

Each student came up one by one and carefully examined each bill and wrote down the letter of the one they selected to be real next to their name on the class roster.

The envelope marked A is wrong. B is the good money.

Three of the girls picked B and none of the boys got it right. I was surprised at the outcome of this little experiment. All three girls said that A was very good, but there was just something about it that they couldn't explain that made them pick B.

I gave the three girls and A, and the rest a B.

"Today we'll look at the paper consistency and features embedded into the paper. There are red and blue fibers in the paper. You'll have to look closely to see them. If you had two counterfeit bills from the same counterfeit run, the fibers would be in the same place."

"This is because some counterfeiters, mostly college kids, make a photo of the bill then make plates from it. The computer will copy the colors correctly, but it can not change their location. This would mean that the colored fibers were always in the same place. And in the natural, that could never happen." I said.

"As you probably already know, the paper that the currency is printed on is twenty five percent linen and seventy five percent cotton. This paper in very hard to purchase, beg, borrow, steal or make."

"Normally it is very easy to feel the difference between real paper and the phony one. Take any piece of paper in one hand and a bill in the other and feel the difference. This is the easiest test for funny money."

Yesterday was the easiest day so far. All the students got it. Today we'll try again.

"The counterfeiters use the serial numbers from ten or more bills over and over. They make one or two million per run, a run takes a day or so. So if you would find two with the same number, you are assured that one is phony. Probably both."

"Embedded in every Federal Reserve note is a clear polyester thread which lists the denomination of the note on the thread. The thread is visible when held up to the light. Each denomination has its own unique position for the thread, and a distinct color when seen in ultraviolet light."

"Has everyone found one of the threads?"
There was a positive response for the threads.

"And last but certainly not least, there is color shifting ink that changes color when viewed from different angles, and the enlarged off-center portrait on the front."

"There are counterfeit detectors in banks, but not all banks have one. Some of the smaller ones aren't equipped quite yet."

"Well, now that you are all experts, do you feel smarter?" I said.

"I have explained and shown you what to look for in the phony bills. Now comes another exercise. I have been notified that there is a ring of counterfeiters operating right here in this city. Since all of you and I have the information about how to find the phony money, I would like for you to try to find out where it is coming from."

"This is not mandatory. If you don't want to do this, there will not be a down grade of any kind. And if you do find something, do NOT intervene. The people who do this see this as their livelihood, and anyone interfering with that is a threat, and threats are disposed of. Do you understand what I am saying?"

This time there was no wishy-washy comments. They said that they understood, loud and clear.

"The semester ends in four weeks. You have two weeks for this project. I will see you all here then. Bring any evidence here and I will act on it as necessary. Remember! Do not post anything to the internet! Almost everyone knows how to find someone from what they post. And you don't want these people to find you."

"Good morning, class."
"Good morning, Mr. Wynn." They said in unison.
"Are we anxious and ready to learn more about money and crooks?"
I immediately got a raised hand and a question for one of them.
"Why would a terrorist be interested in counterfeit money?"
"Because they can deplete a town of all the money in it then say the town is corrupt. If this is the hometown of a prominent politician, they will say he is corrupt. The media will pick it up and blow it all out of proportion and the terrorists win. Again. The terrorist will harp on this supposed fact, which is actually a lie, in order to get their man elected to the position held by our man and take one free politician away from us."
"They will take over the city, county, state or federal offices this way. They need only one bank in the town to succeed at this lie, usually the smallest."
"They put the phony money in the bank by the millions and remove every dollar out of the bank that is possible. The good money then goes into their coffers."

Another day, another fun class. "Good morning class."
"Good morning, Mr. Wynn." They said.

"Money laundering is the world's third largest business.

And also the second chapter in our longer and longer boring lectures." They all laughed and we got started.

"For money laundering to be effective, some basic rules must be followed or all the work will be in vain. Money laundering is the process where the proceeds of a crime are changed into legitimate dollars."

"The ownership and source of the money must be concealed. There's no sense in laundering money if everyone knows who it belonged to and where it originated after it comes out the other end."

"Money from extortion, insider trading, drugs, illegal gambling, or tax evasion, is dirty and needs to be cleaned up to show non criminal activities, in order that banks will deal with it. This money is always overly inflated for book keeping purposes and for looks."

"They must change the form it takes. No one wants to wash three million dollars in twenty dollar bills only to wind up with three million dollars in twenty dollar bills. Changing the form means also reducing the bulk."

"Contrary to popular belief. You cannot stuff one million dollars into an attaché' case, not even a large briefcase. A million dollars in hundreds stands five feet high and weighs over twenty two pounds."

"This is important. The trail left by the process must be hidden and undefined. The whole purpose of money laundering is defeated if someone can follow the money from beginning to end."

"They must have constant control over the process. Most of the people who come into contact with the money being laundered know that it is dirty money, and if they steal it, there's little that the original owner can legally do about it. Keep in mind that word is 'legally', but if they find out, violence may be expected."

"Where does this stuff come from?" Emily asked.

"Drug dealers, extortion, kidnapping, all kinds of criminal activity where money is involved."

"That would be all of it, wouldn't it?" Jean said.

"A drug dealer who accumulates five million dollars in cash is faced with the gigantic task of injecting as many as a quarter of a million pieces of paper into the banking system." I said.

"By moving the money between as many accounts as he can, in and out of dummy companies, relying on bank secrecy, and attorney client privilege to hide his own identity, he tries to create a complex web of financial transactions to frustrate any audit."

"The washed funds are brought back into circulation now in the form of clean and often taxable money. This is one of the main places where the crooks screw up the most. They don't pay the taxes on the money they actually say they are making. Consequently, the IRS gets involved and they go directly to jail."

"Now, if you really want to clean your money, you could do what Amy was doing when we caught her."

I told the story of Amy and her Kenmore laundry. Even before I was finished, most of them were either shocked that someone would do such a thing, or they were laughing so hard that they had to work just to stay in their seats.

Jim too. I had not told him about Amy.

The Bank President finally gave up a name. We would have had it sooner if they would have let me question him. I don't have any qualms about shooting a bank president in the thigh to get the information I want. The problem is that most all the law enforcement folks know it too.

The name we received so graciously from him was Bill Russell.

"You must think that we are as stupid as you are. There isn't a man in this country over the age of twenty who doesn't know who Bill Russell is. You are actually going to try to scam me with this name. Have you ever heard of a game called basketball?"

He sat and looked like he was sulking. I could tell that he hated me, but do I care? Not even a little!

I called Mike to ask him to call Pittsburgh and verify the name.

"Hello, Jeff? This is Mike McCoy. I need a little information. Could you help me?" Mike said.

"Sure Mike. What's up?" Jeff said.

"My friend One Shot McCoy has a suspect telling him that a Bill Russell works the laundry in Salt Lake. Is that true?" Mike said.

"I don't know. Salt Lake is handled through Albuquerque." He said. "I have their phone number right here."

Mike called the Albuquerque number and got Luigi Puzo.

"Hello. This is Lou. What can I do for you?" He said.

"Hello, Lou. This is One Shot McCoy from KC. A friend of mine has someone who's been telling him that there is a guy named Bill Russell that runs the laundry in Salt Lake. Is that the truth?"

"No, not at all. That would be George Coppola. What do you need him for?" He said.

"He has a bank president trying to slide some under the table and we caught him. Now he's blaming someone else."

"Sounds about right. That's what they do. Will you take care of it?"

"I guarantee it!" Mike said.

"Good! Thanks." Lou said.

Chapter 11

Mining For Money

"Good morning, class."

"Good morning, Mr. Wynn." They said in unison.

"Are we anxious and ready to learn more about money and crooks?"

I immediately got a raised hand and a question from one of them.

"Why would anyone bother with money laundering, when they have so much money just laying around?" Alice asked.

"I have always wondered that myself, but there is no way to understand the thinking of another person. Especially if they are a crook or evil of any sort."

"The amount of money laundered in this country is at least a billion dollars per year. So you can see what a big problem it is."

"We found a counterfeiter running a casino that made a million dollars a day. Tell me why he thought he needed to make counterfeit when he already had that rate of income? You can't spend that much money in a day, every day."

"Well, maybe you don't understand the bulk of the money. When you are holding one bill, no matter what denomination it is, it seems very little. But make a pile of twenties to get a couple hundred dollars. Let's multiply that by a hundred. Now you have a pile that you can't carry in your pockets, or even in a briefcase."

"Many methods may be used to accomplish the cleaning of the funds. You could give it to a Service company. That's what I think is happening here. But I don't have any idea who could be doing it, or where it is located."

"You could layer it with legitimate dollars and then integrate it into the normal flow of dollars as a common form. You could try to cover it with complex transactions to cover the source of the funds. You could use smaller amounts to buy dollars, bonds, stocks, all with small deposits, then deposit these again somewhere else."

"You could try to physically transport the money to an off shore account. But, someone might see you and your boat. Or you could get a really big suitcase and go commercial. All of these are not very smart. But they have all been tried."

"You could get involved with a cash intensive business, like a casino, strip club, parking garage or even a tanning bed salon. One thing, this state does not have a casino in it. Not even one. That means that they would have to go to Nevada or Colorado to do their business. We're still not doing very well."

"Several other possibilities come to mind. Trade based companies, shell companies, round tripping. You give money to a law firm as a cash on-account deposit, then cancel the retainer and have the money remitted back to you. Then show the money received as a legacy or possibly proceeds of a court action."

Just then, the Dean walked in.

"Excuse me Mr. Wynn. There's an important call for you in my office. The Dean said.

"Excuse me folks. I'll be right back."

I followed the Dean to his office where his secretary gave me the phone.

"Hello, this is David Wynn."

"We got word that the guy, you remember, the travelling terrorist. He called himself Johnny Cash because the customer had to have cash for him to do the job. Well, he was seen in Salt Lake yesterday." Mike said.

"Have you got a photo?"

"Yeah, I'm sending it now." Mike said.

"I have it. He doesn't look like Johnny Cash."

"What? Oh! No. Not even a little." He said.

"I have a possible here. He's a Professor at the University, and he's missing. I thought this might be him. We've got a lot of craziness going on, and I'm trying to get a handle on something. I'll let you know how we do with this."

"Well class, I must go do something. I'll see you tomorrow. Don't forget to study ahead. You always want to be ahead of the teacher."

The first thing I asked Ray when we reported in was the identities of the seven missing teachers. Then I showed him the photo that Mike sent.

"We identified all seven of them and the one who is missing is James Finch. And wouldn't you know, he teaches Math, Science and Astronomy. It seems to be a trend with these guys." He said.

"We don't know tall, short, white, black, young, or old he is. The only thing we think we know is that our man is a teacher."

"We have looked for the missing teachers and we found seven missing. We investigated all of them. Some are off on vacation, some got another job, some moved away, one of them is our guy." Ray said.

"Did anyone get a list of names of the missing teachers?"

"Yes. I have it here." Ray said.

I wanted to see the names in case I ever saw any of them again. Mathew Bailey, Tyler Hogan, Brady Sanders, Henry Jackson, Alexander Wilson, Robert Woods. I wrote them down in my book.

"So who is the seventh one?"

"His name is James Finch, and we can't find him anywhere. I put out an APB and leaked it to the media." Ray said.

I excused myself for a minute and as I was just walking by when the phone rang, the dispatcher handed it to me and giggled because she caught me unawares. These girls seem to enjoy having fun at my expense.

"Hello, what can I do for you?"

I heard that you wanted information on a teacher named James Finch. I know him and I have just seen him today." She said.

"Where and when did you see him?"

"I was just now coming back from Salt Lake to my house in Park City. There is a road that we never see anyone use going out to some old abandoned mines.

That is where we saw them. There were two of them in an old car." She said.

"I hope you have a photo of him. None of us knows what he looks like. I'll come right up there if you do."

"I should have one. I have a copy of last year's University Annual somewhere." She said.

She gave me her home address and phone number and directions to find her house. She said she would be waiting.

One thing I learned a long time ago was this. I don't go into the forests here in the west without my IR glasses. Infrared glasses pick up any heat left my animals and people who have been in that place. Better than that is this. When it is dark and someone is in the area, the glasses will show a glow from their body heat.

"I'm on my way."

Jim and I raced up the hill to Park City to the address the woman gave me. Jim knocked on the door and she answered immediately.

A nice looking woman about twenty three came to the door.

"Debbie, I'm David Wynn. We spoke earlier about James Finch."

"Yes. Won't you come in?" She said.

She had the University Annual laying out on the dining room table.

"I thought you would want to see this. There are many pictures of the faculty and staff here. This one is James Finch." She pointed to the man in one of the photos.

"That's not the guy in the photo that Mike sent me."

"He doesn't look like a terrorist. Actually neither one of them do. This guy is old and gray and wears glasses." Jim said.

"We don't know that he is yet. We need to find him. He might be a terrorist or he may be in trouble with a real crook or terrorist."

"What are you studying at the University, Debbie?"

"I started in Criminal Justice and now I am taking a few courses in Legal Studies. I don't know whether I want to be a Lawyer or in Law Enforcement." She said.

"When you decide call me, I will probably have a job for you. You know, I might like to use you in a project that I think will be coming up soon." I handed her one of my cards.

"Great! I would enjoy a little action." She said.

I gave Debbie all the information on Lieutenant Ray and the PD.

"If you call him, be sure to use my name as a reference. I think you may have found your calling here."

"If Finch is the guy we want, you need to know that he is armed and dangerous. He shoots people. That's how we know where he is. We have tried to catch him in Kansas City, Colorado Springs, and now here. We know he has been seen, or his work has, all over the Southwest."

Jim and I jumped in our car and sped off in the direction of the mine that Debbie told us about. She was right about a dusty dirty dirt road, but in only a few minutes we saw the mine buildings and stopped. We backed the car into and under some trees in hopes that it would be hidden if someone came while we were inside.

Jim and I walked into the building. It looks exactly like what you would expect a hundred year old wooden mine building to look like. Old, dirty, unkempt and unused. There was an old wooden table with two chairs around it in the middle of the room.

There was no electricity, but there was a cast iron wood stove off to the side. It was cold, so we know it has been some time since there was anyone here. There were two beds, that is, mattresses, and a safe. Everything covered with dust.

"We've been in this place before. Every time we had a meeting with the drug dealers and all the other crooks back home. I wonder why they all like the dirty, crappy places to stay?"

We think this is where the occupants have their office and they have meetings. It looks like the crooks have made their hideout in an old abandoned gold mine, but not this one.

I brought the IR binoculars with me, and when I scanned the area for residue, there wasn't even a glimmer. It looks like no one has been here in a long time.

The tracks are still in the tunnels, there are a few mine cars sitting around and the tracks lead out to a small wooden building.

"Who are they? Let's go look in the mine, maybe we'll get a clue there." Jim said.

We walked out of their office and into the mine tunnel opening. It is really a dark tunnel with metal railroad tracks in the center. Just what you would expect in a mine tunnel.

I suddenly got the feeling like we are being followed by someone, but we don't know who. Every once in a while we think we heard a sound, but when we look for it, there is nothing there.

We both have our guns in hand for defense, but we don't know what to defend against. It is spooky. Suddenly I found what feels like a door and I opened it, but there was only a very small room with no furniture or facilities there.

I went into the room while Jim waited outside in case someone should come.

I scoured that room with my hands, the flashlight and the IR glasses. Found nothing! I checked the ceiling and the floor and all the walls.

"I can't find anything in here Jim. You want to try, and I'll stand guard?"

"OK." Jim said and we switched places.

Jim spent almost fifteen minutes doing the same thing I did. He didn't find anything either. We decided to put a stakeout on the place when we get back to town.

Lieutenant Ray authorized a stakeout for the mine. We contacted the phone company and they let us use one of their trucks. We parked it next to a pole near the dirt road turnoff. Jim and I took turns being outside pretending that we were working on the phone lines.

Fortunately after about eight hours, we were relieved by two officers from the division. I was really glad, it had been a long day. It's time for Jim and I to go back and get some rest and a bite to eat.

I made a special trip to the Director's office to see Fred Martin. He is the senior agent in the area.

"Ya know. Now that Mr. Flynn is out of the way, you might want to do the OUR BANK thing like I did back in KC when we had the Money Launderers use the bank for their money. I will give you every detail about how it will work."

"I have a friend who is a real estate agent here. I have talked to him about buying an old building. He thinks there are several around town which are closed and could be bought for almost nothing." Fred said.

"Why can't you use the bank on Fifteenth South?"

"Why a bank?" He said.

"What better place to keep money?"

"How did you get the crooks to buy your story?" He asked.

"Back in KC the crooks saw me as one of them. I think I convinced them that our bank was the perfect way to launder their money and distribute the counterfeit as well."

"I like the sound of that. That sounds like a good idea." He said.

"We could have agents posing as tellers. If you want to be the Bank President, you might need to be thought of as a crook by the money men."

I explained in detail all of the tricks I did to fool them into believing I was the real deal. "It took awhile, but I did it."

"Once I was arrested and put in jail, I had them. After we got the bank ready and open for business, I called Perry and had him come to see what I could do for him. I gave him a tour of everything including the vault. From that time on we had two of his men making deliveries twice a week."

"I told you about Amy and the equipment we had to buy and install in the bank basement. You might not have to go to the lengths that we did, but it was always fun going to work in the morning. Let's go look at the building and you and your agents can decide what you want to do."

Chapter 12

A Stakeout

"I already closed that bank on Fifteenth South. We'll use it till something comes up or someone who owns it finds out what we're doing. Maybe you could buy it. Or I could."

"I really like that idea! We could clean it up and suddenly be in business. I like it!" Fred said.

"I will need some help having someone make me a crook for all the other crooks to see." He said.

"How about this? We could catch you on the street and handcuff and arrest you in broad daylight and tell the press that we caught a notorious counterfeiter and money launderer from back east. They probably wouldn't check. But if they did we could backstop it with our friends at the FBI."

"Counterfeiting is what we want, but that's not enough for a display like this. Is it? He asked.

"They got me with a gun charge. It was easy. I always have a gun with me."

"I carry a gun most of the time, but mine isn't as fancy as yours. Would the Director and the police go along with all this?" He asked.

"Only one way to find out!"

"Oh man! I hate it when you do that to me." He said.

The Director was enthusiastically in favor of our whole plan.

We went with Fred to see Lieutenant Ray and we laid out our plan for Fred to be seen as a crook. He loved the idea and said that he would help in any way he could. Just call him ahead of the need.

It was getting on toward evening and I just had to drive up the hill again. We have had this road to the mine staked out for nearly a week with no success.

"Wait! Look! I've seen that car before. Quick Jim get a picture of it and the plate."

It's a good thing we didn't have anything laying out on the ground in front of the truck. I fired it up and began to follow the car.

The car only drove to the next dirt road up the hill and turned off and drove into the forest. Do you mean that we have been here for a week and watching the wrong road? I feel like such a fool.

Jim and I parked the truck and went on foot following the car into the woods. We walked most of a mile back into the woods until we saw another mine with another old wooden building and some mine cars sitting around it just like the other one. But no civilian car.

We quietly slinked up to the building and peeked in. No one home! No car! No tracks! I don't get it. Neither of us said a word. We scoured the ground for signs of people or vehicles. Nothing! I took out the IR glasses and found shiny residue all around where we were standing. You can't tell if the shine was left by a person or an animal.

There were tracks in the dirt road, but way too many to tell what was happening around here. I could see lots of heat evidence here, but it's too sketchy to be good for us. I couldn't get a full figure in the glasses, but I can tell there has been a lot of warm traffic around here.

"There's been a few people here, but I can't tell when."

"We're going to have to turn this over to the next shift. We have things to do today, remember?" He said.

"You're right. Let's go. We'll come back when it's dark. Maybe we'll have more luck then with the glasses."

"If they're not here, where are they? We just saw them drive in.

"Maybe the next mine down the road? If there is one." Jim said.

"We need a smaller vehicle. That truck is way too big. Even our car is too big, but it's better."

I mentioned it to Ray when we got back and he said that one of the people there had an old VW that maybe we could use. The owner said that she would be glad to let us use it.

The next day we were just driving around town being tourists when we saw our travelling terrorist come out of a drug store to the street.

"Hey! There's our terrorist getting in that car." Jim said.

"Hurry! Let's follow him."

We made sure we were way back at a safe distance and followed him from the drug store to the

University where he stopped and went into a build-ing for about ten minutes. We took a photo of the building and I wrote down the building number and street name.

Next we are off to the Fort, where we stopped again for about ten minutes. And I wrote down all the pertinent information.

Next, up the hill to Park City where he stopped at a white house trimmed in blue. I wrote the address and the name on the mailbox, Elliot.

I called Ray and gave him all the details we came up with. I hope he can put some meat onto what we gave him.

I have a class today and I have got to study for a few minutes so I can get this right. It took a while for me to find where I had left off with the calls yester-day. I probably will have to start over to get it right.

I was right! I had to start over because I lost my train of thought when Mike called. The class loved it and they had a good time for most of the class about it.

"I think we're having too much fun here today. Let's postpone this until tomorrow."

They all agreed and I dismissed the class.

Jim and I took the little old VW and went into the forest to try to find whatever was in there waiting for us.

This is the Wasatch Mountains. Still part of the Rockies, but different in so many ways. This is the westernmost face of the range. It gets more rain, more snow, and more sun than the front range in Colorado. Consequently the forests are thicker and darker. It's only six in the evening and the sun is going down. I'm glad I have the IR glasses, we'll need them.

I drove to the third mine down the road and stopped to scan the area with the glasses. I picked up a little more reflections than I had before, so I parked the car under a tree and we began to inspect the place.

Once again, it feels like we are being followed by someone, but we don't know who. It's a funny feeling that's hard to put your finger on. Every once in a while we think we heard a sound but when we look for it there is nothing there. We both have our guns in hand for defense. But we don't know what to defend against. It is spooky.

There are mines all over the Rockies. The crooks have made their hideout in a mine somewhere. There are a few mine cars sitting around this one and the tracks lead out of the mine to a small wooden bldg just like all the others.

I was standing next to Jim scanning the forest when I caught two bright shadows rising up behind Jim. I tapped him and pointed to the men as I pulled James Bond out of his resting place.

One of them fired.

"BANG!"

And I fired.

"Physstt!"

I was hit in the chest on the left shoulder. I missed! How could I miss? I never miss! While I was thinking that I never miss, I fell on the ground.
"Whump!"
I'm sure glad he did miss. It's a good thing I had the vest on. The shot knocked me down, but Jim spun around and shot both of them and called 911 for support.

"Physstt!" "Physstt!"

"Boy! That really hurts!"
Jim gave Ray good directions and we waited for them to arrive. Jim finally got around to helping me get up off of the ground. Boy! It still hurts!
After the squad picked up the bodies and cleaned up the area, Jim said he would take me to a doctor in Park City. I told him to look for a Chiropractor.
We took off my vest and holster in the woods and put them in the trunk before going to the doctor. We don't need any more notoriety. We found that my left shoulder was bruised really bad and I was having a lot of pain even though the vest stopped the bullet. It was starting to turn colors. I couldn't see them very well, but Jim mentioned red and purple.

"Hello, I'm Dr. Mason, What can I do for you?" She said.

"My friend here had a fall today and hurt his shoulder. I hoped you could relieve the pain and help it to heal." Jim said.

"Yes I think I can do that." She said.

"OK, take your shirt off and over on your stomach. My! You have a big bruise." She began to feel for broken bones and things that were out of place. "Wow!" Does that hurt!

"Crick." "Ouch!" "Crack." "Ouch!" "Crack." "Oof!"

"Now on your right side."

It was all I could do to move around on the doctor's table.

Twist. "Crick." "Ouch!" Turn. "Crack." "Oh!"

"It's getting better." She said. "Now on your left side."

Twist. "Clack!" "Umm!"

"Now sit up."

Twist. "Snap!" "Ahh!"

"There! That's the one." She said.

"Your left shoulder was dislocated. I had to give it room to go back in the right place." She said. "Now I think you are back in place. Don't do any more funny exercises."

Something told me that she knew that the bruises and pain were not from a fall. But she didn't say anything and I did the same.

Suddenly a large part of the pain flew out the window. I felt like I was going to live. I thanked her several times, took one of her business cards, paid her for the visit and walked out of her office like an almost normal person, but Jim drove back to town.

We still don't know who belongs to the name on the mysterious notebook. Was it a student, when did it get written, was it a teacher, or a professor, or a spy, we don't know anything. I hope there are latent prints on it. I took it to the lab some time ago. I need to see them and find out what they found.

Chapter 13

Money Matters

It was a long hard night, but here it is morning and soon it will be time to go to class and pretend that everything is alright. I need to finish the class I botched up so badly the other day. I didn't know it, but I was favoring my left arm.

"Good morning, class. Let's go back and go over the part that leads up to where we are now. I got a little off track yesterday."

"I notice that you are favoring your left arm, sir. Have you hurt it?" Susanne said.

"Yes. I took a fall yesterday and I had to go see a chiropractor. I can recommend this doctor to you, she really is great! But now I'm a lot better." I showed them the doctor's business card.

I had to go back and go over the part that leads up to this part where we are now.

"I may have said this before but stay with me.

"The amount of money laundered in this country is at least a billion dollars per year. So you can see what a big problem it is. Many methods may be used to accomplish the cleaning of the funds. You could give it to a Service company. That's what I think is happening here."

"For money laundering to be effective, some basic rules must be followed or all the work will be in vain.

Money laundering is the process where the proceeds of a crime is changed into legitimate dollars."

"The ownership and source of the money must be concealed. There's no sense in laundering money if everyone knows who it belonged to and where it originated after it comes out the other end."

"Money from extortion, insider trading, drugs, illegal gambling, or tax evasion, is dirty and needs to be cleaned up to show non criminal activities, in order that banks will deal with it. This money is always overly inflated for book keeping purposes and for looks."

"They must change the form it takes. No one wants to wash ten million dollars in hundreds only to wind up with the same ten million dollars in hundreds again. Changing the form means also reducing the bulk. Do you realize that a million dollars in hundreds stands five feet high and weighs over twenty two pounds?"

"This is important. The trail left by the process must be hidden and undefined. The whole purpose of money laundering is defeated if someone can follow the money from beginning to end."

"They must have constant control over the process. Most of the people who come into contact with the money being laundered know that it is dirty money, and if they steal it, there's little that the original owner can legally do about it. Keep in mind that word is 'legally', but if they find out, violence will definitely be expected very soon after the discovery of the shortage."

"A drug dealer who accumulates five million dollars in cash is faced with the gigantic task of injecting as many as a quarter of a million pieces of paper into the banking system."

"By moving the money between as many accounts as he can, in and out of dummy companies, relying on bank secrecy, and attorney client privilege to hide his own identity, he tries to create a complex web of financial transactions to frustrate any audit."

"All of these people have lawyers on retainer in case of any problems."

"The washed funds are brought back into circulation now in the form of clean and often taxable money. This is one of the main places where the crooks screw up the most. They don't pay the taxes on the money they actually say they are making legally. Consequently, the IRS gets involved and they go to jail.

"You could layer it with legitimate dollars and then integrate it into the normal flow of dollars as a common form. You could try to cover it with complex transactions to cover the source of the funds. You could use smaller amounts to buy dollars, bonds, stocks, even gold, all with small deposits, then deposit these again somewhere else. By the way, gold is very heavy."

"You could try physically transporting the money to an off shore account. But, someone might see you and your boat. Or get a really big suitcase and go commercial. All of these are not very smart."

"You could get involved with a cash intensive business, like a casino, strip club, parking garage or even a tanning bed place. We're still not doing very well. There are no casinos in this state. That means they would have to physically transport it to a bordering state like Nevada or Colorado to get rid of it."

"Several other possibilities come to mind. Trade based companies, shell companies, round tripping. You could give money to a law firm as a cash-on-account deposit, then cancel the retainer and have the money remitted back to you. Then show the money received as a legacy or proceeds of a court action. But how many times do you think the law firms would put up with that?"

There's a few others, real estate comes to mind. You buy a house to flip, buy it with dirty money and do a quick flip. A quick flip could take several weeks and more physical labor than you want to put out. Then get clean money after the sale."

"The seller could under value the house and once it is sold, get a check which would be clean money as it is deposited. Fictitious loans, credit cards at a tax haven bank, like OUR BANK."

"Keep in mind that if you are doing this kind of business, you are on the wrong side of the law and jail is always looming in your future."

It was a good class and I think they're finally getting it. Now it's time for Jim and I to check in to the Station.

We got a call from one of the fire stations that a terrorist with a bomb in a suitcase was going into a fire station.

"He has been yelling that we destroyed his house. He said that he has a bomb and is going to destroy ours." The Chief said.

Ray called us and told Jim and I to take this call. I really didn't want to run another call because of my shoulder, but someone had to do it. Jim parked down the street from the Firehouse and on the other side so we didn't look threatening to him.

He was seventy five or eighty yards away from us when we found him. There were only five or six cars in the lot on the other side. Jim had his binoculars in his hand trying to get a good look at him. Jim yelled at him. He turned and aimed his gun at us and fired one off.

"Well if that's the way he wants it, I'm ready."

All I had with me was James Bond, so that had to do.

Jim knelt down on the ground to make himself a smaller target. I had to get down on the ground on my stomach. This was just like being at the doctor. Except I'm the one who is going to stop the pain. I held the pistol close to me under my chin so no one could see it.

I took careful aim and fired my hundred yard shot at it.

"Physstt!"

I knew what was coming and I slid the pistol under me and buried my face in the grass.

"Baarroooommm!"

The suitcase blew up like a small atomic bomb. The shock wave blew dust and dirt in every direction. Jim was down on one knee when it blew, and it knocked him on his back, There was no damage to the parking lot except all the windows in the fire house and all the cars were suddenly gone. And of course our suitcase carrier was also gone.

The next day some of the people in the class had the daily paper and they asked me where I was yesterday.

"Jim and I were out shopping."

"Look at this." She said.

It seems that some nosy photographer took my picture when I was confronting the suitcase guy. There we were, Jim and I, in the paper on the front page of the second section. Damn! The paper only said 'unnamed law enforcement personnel'. At least the photo didn't show a gun, or my face.

"Who are you really?" She said.

"You didn't think that I was an accounting geek, did you?"

"No, but you're not really a teacher then are you?" Emily said.

"Oh yes, I am very much a teacher."

"What do you teach?" She said.

"Well, of course, there is the thing about money. I have taught this course many times. Usually without all the distractions."

"Yes?" She said.

"But more importantly, I have taught several terrorists that we won't be moved."

"Then I teach living. There are people who don't want us to be living. It is my job to teach these terrorists that we will continue to live here whether they like it or not."

I had to stop the question and answer period, so I did.

"Now that you know a little more about me that I did not want anyone to know, what do you think about our problem?"

A boy in the back row stood up and said. "If you are going to teach us all of this about money and keep the bad guys away from us, I'm all for you. I will do anything I can to help."

The whole class held up their hands and said that they agreed with him.

"Good! I have a need for some information, and some of you might be able to get it for me."

"I saw this man enter building 403 two days ago." I showed them the only photo of Johnny Cash the Terrorist I had.

"I want to know who he is, who he is seeing, where I can find him, anything that will give me a start with him. He has stopped at this building at the school for about ten minutes. I need to know who he talked to and how to find them."

"He also stopped at a building on Soldiers Circle. Same stuff.

"The last thing is a house in Park City with Elliot on the mailbox. I put all the information I had on the board so they could copy what they wanted."

"He is called the Travelling Terrorist. He kills people and no one knows how to stop him. I thought I would try my hand."

"You think you can stop him?" One asked.

"Well I do have this." I pulled out James Bond. "And he doesn't know me. That gives me the advantage. However I have been told that he will shoot anyone that comes close to him just for fun."

It was a bad week, Mike called about the Travelling Terrorist. We saw him but we lost him. We have a missing teacher. We know who he is but not where he is, or if he is in trouble or part of the trouble.

I got shot. I saw a chiropractor and she put me back together like a jigsaw puzzle. The pain slowed down but it's still there.

I tried to teach class but got interrupted. Then I lost all my thoughts. Now I'm back in class trying to pick it back up and get to normal.

I had talked about the OUR BANK story during our discussions. The class thought it would be a great idea and all of them wanted to help. How am I going to explain this? I can't let a bunch of civilians take on a dangerous job like that. They are not agents or even law enforcement.

All of a sudden the classroom door burst open and a man came charging through.

"Who the hell do you think you are?" He shouted.

It was a guy I had never seen before waving his arms and acting threatening. He came at me and I stepped out of the way and he fell over my desk. When he got to his feet, I was standing there with James Bond ready to pick his nose for him.

"Who wants to know?"

He stopped ranting and got a good look at my friend.

"You threw my son out of school and they arrested him." He said.

"From your rant you obviously don't know who I am. I am called One Shot McCoy. I shoot bad guys. You are now climbing the ladder of my patience and could soon be nominated for that honor. Now sit and tell me what this is all this about."

He went on a little until I figured out that he was the loud-mouth kid's dad. I told the class to tell him what happened that day. The dad was shocked and not happy at what they said.

"From his reaction about the phone, I think he is a terrorist or at least a sympathizer. You had better get some psychological help for him. If he comes at one of us with a gun he will find a concrete bed waiting for him in the morgue. We don't put up with that stuff anymore."

I put James Bond in his place and showed the man the door.

The class was shocked but silent.

"That's what I do."

Chapter 14

The Federal Reserve System

I made it a point to get to class very early today. I know there will be some feelings and questions flying around and I want to head them off if I can. I took my seat and leaned back in a relaxed pose as they walked in.

One by one they looked at me, smiled and sat. I could tell that someone wanted to say something, but none of them knew where to start. I waited until all of them were seated and they were deciding what to say.

"What would you like to know?"

That broke the ice. There were four or five of them all talking at the same time.

"We just want to know who are you, really?" She said.

"Well, you showed me the paper and asked if that was me in the photo. Yes it was. We got a call from someone, and we went to try to stop something terrible from happening. We did."

"How did you do that? You were very far from the man with the bomb. We didn't hear a gunshot." He said.

"How many of you own a pistol? We don't say 'gun' when anyone can hear the word."

All the hands went up.

"How many of you can hit a target in the center at twenty-five or fifty yards?"

Half of the hands went down.

"Of those left, how many of you can hit a target at seventy-five to a hundred yards?"

One hand was left. It was a girl!

"Come up here. You are my student for one day. I have something to show you, then you can pass it on to the others here, then they will know how it happens."

Gloria smiled and sat in the chair next to my desk.

"Now let's get on with what is the next most important part of your study of money. There is a Federal Reserve Bank here in town. You need to know how it works. If you actually are going to be in banking, this will be important to you. If not, it will just be a point of interest for you."

"I have contacted the bank and they have agreed to a guided tour through their facility. I must call back to confirm the date and time. It will take some time, but today is not the day. I can tell there are more questions bubbling up."

"What is your name?" One asked.

"When I am in Salt Lake, my name is David Wynn. When I am in another town, I have a different name."

"Who is One Shot McCoy?" Another asked.

"A name I have used in the Midwest where I was thought to be a crook."

"Are you a cop?" Another asked.

"I have been called a lot of names, most of them are bad. I suppose cop was in there sometime."

"Have you shot many people?" Another asked.

"A few."

"What kind of people were they?" One asked.

"Drug dealers, traitors, terrorists, gang members and cartel members. Just a mix of abnormal people in this country."

"Would you have shot that man who was here yesterday?" Emily asked.

"Only if he had threatened the life of someone in this room or this school. Without hesitation!"

One girl stood and pointed at Jim. "Is he really your nephew?" She asked.

"No, actually he is my partner. We have been together for some time now. He covers my back. He is the reason that I can still walk."

"How would I get a job like what you do?" He asked.

"Here is a partial list of requirements. A degree in Criminal Justice, some knowledge of Legal Studies wouldn't hurt, handy with firearms of various kinds, a little martial arts wouldn't hurt, and maybe a specialty of some kind that might make you an expert, like finance or something in technology."

"We all know that you carry a gun. Is it something special and is it there all the time?" One asked.

I call it James Bond. If you have ever seen the Bond movies you know what it is. And yes, every day, all day long."

"I've given you all more than I have ever revealed to anyone before. I hope I won't regret it. Now I would like to go with this girl to the shooting range. You should think about the Fed that we are going to visit and also how to keep a very important secret from everyone you know as well as everyone that you don't know."

"We will talk about the Fed a little before we make the visit tomorrow. You all have the books I handed out. While you study those today and tomorrow, Gloria and I will take a trip to the shooting range. See you tomorrow."

Jim, Gloria and I drove to a shooting range she knew about near the Fort and I went through all the little intricacies of the hundred yard shot with her. The caliber of the bullet, the weight, the speed of it and gravity. She tried it several times until she got the feel of it and hit it. She was elated.

"I didn't think it was possible! I did it! I am in your debt." She said.

"You owe me nothing. Only that you can become the best that you can be. I hope to see you around the office sometime."

I called the Fed for a date and time and everyone in the class said that they would be ready to go at the appointed time. Two people, guards, from the Federal Reserve Bank met us in the lobby. They introduced themselves and took the class on the guided tour. Jim and I stood around until a man who said he was the Bank President came over to us and asked who we were.

I reached into my jacket without showing him James Bond and pulled out my badge. Jim did the same.

"I didn't know we rated this high. We don't see many of you guys around." He said.

I explained about the counterfeit and money laundering and why we were in town. I also explained my name and about the class.

"You guys really do things up right. I had no idea there was this much interest in banking in this town." He said.

Once the tour was over, the two guards returned the class to me with their complements about their conduct and observance of the posted rules. They were all smiles when we left.

"Now that the tour is finished, you have the little hundred page book they gave you, I'll bet it feels like a thousand. I suggest that you familiarize yourself with it and we will talk about it for the next several days."

"Good morning everybody. Do you understand everything in the little eight and a half by eleven monster they gave you?" - - - - "I didn't think so. What you need is to break down the bankers and lawyers words into your kind of language. Let me show you."

"From the cover of Section One. The Federal Reserve, The Fed, performs five key functions, does things, in the public interest, for us, to promote the health, to help, the US economy of this country, our money, and the stability, permanence, of the US financial system. There now, that wasn't so hard was it?"

They all laughed and began saying out loud "GEEK."

"Here are some more for you to practice on before you get bogged down in the meat of the book. The cover of Section Two. Page twenty-seven, How

Monetary Policy Affects the Economy. Page fifty-six, What is Financial Stability? Page seventy-four, Regulation versus Supervision. And lastly, page ninety, the only paragraph on the page."

"If you can successfully decipher these, you are on your way to becoming a great banker."

"We will move on to other pressing items next week. Be sure to get with Gloria. She has some shocking things to show you."

"Here we go again!"

"Today we will start with Section Two of the Federal Reserve Book. The Three Key System Entities, the Board of Governors, the Federal Reserve Banks and the FOMC."

"Can I get someone to tell us what this is all about?"

Janice stood up and explained in plain language the contents of the section.

"Good job! That is worth an A in any class."

"Now let's move on to Section Three. The Federal Open Market Committee sets US monetary policy in accordance with its mandate from Congress. To promote maximum employment, stable prices and moderate long-term interest rates in the US economy."

"How many of you read this section?"

A few hands went up and I picked one. One of the brighter students gave a very understandable oral report on Section Three. I marked him an A and he sat down.

"One more section and we'll call it a day. Do I have a volunteer?"

The same boy was the only one.

"Section Four." He was reading this time. "The Federal Reserve monitors financial system risk and engages at home and abroad to help ensure the system supports a healthy economy for US households, communities and businesses."

"Very good, Doug! It looks like we have a banker in our midst. I would venture to say that if you follow this route, Doug, you will be first in your class from now on."

"That's enough for today. By the way, you slackers who haven't read any of this, you should at least look at the pictures."

They all laughed and the bell rang right on time.

Around two in the afternoon, I received a call from the Springs. It was Lopez.

"Hello. This is David."

"David who? I was calling for DJ." He said.

"Hello Lopez. David Wynn is the name I'm using here in Salt Lake. What's up?"

"We have been following a few known crazies for a few weeks, and we caught one trying to explode a bomb in an electronics company in Arvada. He had a gun and he waved it at us." Lopez said.

"And of course he was shot by one of your men."

"Yes. But only once. We wouldn't want to sully the reputation of One Shot McCoy, would we?" Lopez said and laughed.

I even laughed at that one.

"Jim and I were told that the Traveling Terrorist was seen here. We saw him once but lost him. He's pretty slippery. But if he stays here, we'll get him."

Lopez and I talked for about a half an hour and he had to go. I'll call him when I have something.

"We only have three more sections of the Federal Reserve book to cover. I hope you read some of it. Who wants to start?"

Adrienne surprised me and stood up and began to read the cover page of Section Five.

"The Federal Reserve promotes the safety and soundness of individual financial institutions and monitors their impact on the financial system as a whole." She said.

"I really liked this section because it says that someone is looking out for our banks. It was very interesting. I had not thought about banking as a career until now, but maybe." She said.

"Who wants to tell us about Section Six?

They all began to try to get one of the boys to do it. He is a bashful kid and doesn't participate in the class orally very often. They kept after him until he finally gave in and began to read the cover page of Section Six.

Then I realized why he relented. It is one of the shortest of them.

"The Federal Reserve works to promote a safe, efficient and accessible system for US dollar transactions." He said.

He had obviously read the section and explained it very well in plain language. But he was shaking the whole time. Once he was finished he quickly sat and was still and quiet. I feel sorry for him. I wish I knew what I could do for him.

"OK. I'll read the last section and we're done with this part of the class. Section Seven, The Federal Reserve advances supervision, community reinvestment and research to increase understanding of the impacts of financial services policies and practices on consumers and communities."

"I've already taught you how to decipher these words, so this one should be one of the easiest."

We went through it in detail and they all laughed at nearly every phrase.

Time to go back to work.

Chapter 15

The Traveling Terrorist

One of the Officers in the Salt Lake PD called the office and said he had seen the Traveling Terrorist on the south side of town coming out of a café. Jim and I immediately ran for the door.

I have been to Salt Lake many times, but I have not seen it rain like it is now. It's coming down in buckets. Jim got the weather on his phone while I piloted our 1962 racing machine toward the south side of town. The Pontiac has a big engine in it and will probably do eighty miles per hour all day long, but in this rain fifty is too fast.

We knew that he had a rental car and the make, model and color. But that's all we had besides his photo. The Officer gave me the name of the café, so we went there first.

I don't know how it happened, but we saw a car like the description we had down the street at a gas station. I got as close as I could and Jim took a photo of the license plate and sent it to the office. An immediate response came back.

'That's the one!"

We followed him from the city streets, south through Murray, out to the Interstate, south to Sandy and farther on to Draper. The weather forecast was as bad as I had ever seen it around here. Salt Lake doesn't get bad weather. They get snow and some rain in the winter and spring, but not like this.

It seems that a big cold front came in from the Pacific and was blasting the mountain states with unseasonal rain. It came against the western slope of the Rockies and rested there. The rain didn't look like it was going to slow down any time soon.

Our man turned off the Interstate and drove into Draper. The rain got so hard and fast that streets began to flood. It was hard to see even with the wipers on full speed. There were cars and trucks stopped in all the intersections of the streets where it was flooding.

Our guy drove right into one of those intersections at normal speed and his car suddenly stopped. He's not as smart as he thinks he is.

"Here's our chance!" Said Jim.

I pulled up into someone's front yard and stopped the car and we bailed out on the front lawn.

He must have made us earlier and he charged into the flooded intersection at a normal speed trying to get away from us. Just to show how dumb these terrorists are, he got stopped by the water so he exited the car and began to shoot at us.

He was up to his waist in water and he is shooting at us. There is only Fire Department and rescue personnel around him and he is shooting at them too.

Jim and I are out of the water in that front yard. I wanted to shoot the clown, but Jim did too. So we flipped a coin to see who would get to shoot him. Jim won. Darn it!

Jim knelt down and pulled out his James Bond and put one in the terrorist's chest. He slid back and down then rose to the top and began to float away. The Firemen threw a rope over the body and pulled it to dry land.

All of this was caught on camera by a nosy TV news reporter. And wouldn't you know, she had the balls to run over to us and try to ask some stupid questions with a live mic and the camera rolling.

"Who are you? What are you two doing? Do you know that you just shot that guy?" She said.

"And now, we are arresting you. And your photographer." The photographer was still rolling. The Chief will love this.

"You can't do that. The Constitution provides for free speech." She was getting loud. I was pulling her arm back to put the handcuffs on and she was fighting me with every move.

"It doesn't say free invasion of speech. You are both under arrest."

By this time Jim had the photographer in handcuffs and his camera was safely in the trunk of our car.

"You can't do this. It's unconstitutional." She was yelling now.

"Yes I can. Would you like to see my badge?"

One of the Firemen came over to us and I showed him my badge. He said. "Boy, are we glad you came along! That guy was shooting at us and he hit one of the cars only a few feet from one of my men. Which one of you got him?"

We told him what we did, and he laughed. "You flipped a coin?"

"He always gets to have all the fun. I thought it was only fair, and I won." Jim said.

He introduced himself to us and asked us about the two in handcuffs.

"This is one of those TV reporters that never knows when they should leave things alone. She was filming our shot of that terrorist."

"He was a terrorist?" The Fireman said.

"Yeah! We've been on his tail for months and we finally caught him here."

"I didn't know!" She said.

"Yes! There are a lot of things that you don't know!"

"We will take the two of you back to the Chief and see what he has to say to you. We will abide by whatever he decides. I suggest that you do the same."

"You might not like what he says, he's a tough old bird. I've known him for twenty years." The Fireman said. "We'll take the body to the Salt Lake morgue, and bring up the TV car."

When we got back to town, the first thing to do was introduce the TV girl to the Chief. We explained what we did and didn't leave out any details. Then we hot-footed it out of there while the Chief had a little talk with the girl and her photog.

As soon as we got back to town and away from the Station, I called Fred Martin for a meeting.

"Do you really want to do the thing with the bank?"

"Yes! I think I can make it work here and maybe break the back of the counterfeiters at the same time." He said.

"I would like to explain everything about our Foundation."

Jim and I sat with him and explained in great detail all about the Foundation, what it does and how it does it. I also explained what we did with OUR BANK in Kansas City. He was all for it.

"The biggest person you will need here is a man or a shop that will do the repairs and put out a good running product for the people. I don't know enough people here to help you with it."

"Don't forget this. I do not want my name mentioned to anyone or near anyone that could hear you!"

"You must know that you can't do this alone, and Jim and I will not be here to help you. You can call us, but that might not answer your question."

"I will fish around for help. How many will I need for this?" He asked.

"Here's a list of what we have. Lawyer, Treasurer, Security, Cyber Security, Public Relations, Police, and you get to do the Details. If you get it started, we will fund the Foundation and the bank."

"Not bad. I think I can do it." He said.

"Now about the bank. I only used experienced agents at every job there. They were tellers, loan officers, a guard without a gun, and all the others. I was in as Bank President. What a joke! The only thing I did was watch for the guys with the suitcases who brought the money."

"We will put a small office in the back for the Foundation. You should have plenty of room in the vault to sort and arrange the money. Remember, if there is counterfeit, it must be put where no one can get it."

"One thing that is a problem, and you will have to give this one some thought. When you have your grand opening, there will be regular people inside the bank. They might even be customers. You can't turn them away. How would that look? And what if your crooks saw you turning people away?"

"One more problem. We will need to keep two of the civilian tellers for looks. They will know the regular customers and they will know her."

We went on with all the details that we could for another hour. Fred feels and thinks that they can do this. I hope he's right.

"I'm ready to get started. What do we do first?" He said.

"Now let's go see the Auto Repair Shop."

Fred drove to a little car lot in Taylorsville. He said the owner was a school friend from years ago. It's a big lot with a small building that looks like a gas station.

"Hi, Brad. I came to tell you about the project we talked about. This is David Wynn. David, this is Bradley Porter." Fred said.

"What is it that you do and what can I do?" He asked.

I explained the car and truck replacement program to him. He was suddenly very interested.

"All cars and trucks will go through your shop. That way we will know what their condition is before we give them to someone else." I said. "I will pay overtime if we need to."

"If the vehicle body is good, we will put a sign on it saying date, make, model, and bad part, and store it in the back of the building. We can fix the ones with a good body and only a few problems. Bad and broken parts will go to be melted down or recycled. Take all the old cars to be used as parts, or fixed, or junked. The rest will go to the crusher or a recycler." Fred said.

"How many vehicles do you think you can get ready in a month, Brad?"

"Easily one a week if they aren't too bad." He said. "But I'll have guys working on them every day." He said.

"Let me call Mark. He usually knows where to find things like this." He said.

"Hello, Mark? Say, I'm going to need a big building and some mechanics to work on cars and parts." He said to Mark.

"We'll save all the good parts, and be sure to tag them and put them on a shelf for future use." He said to me.

"Do you happen to know anyone who might have a building that we could move in here?" He asked Mark.

"I think there's a company in Ogden that sells metal buildings. I'll call and get an estimate." Mark said.

"Sure, it could be a metal building that was too big for anyone to use. - - That'd be great. - - I'll be here, let me know as soon as you can. - - - Thanks Mark." He said.

"Mark said he knew about something, but he'd have to check on it. He'll call me." Fred said.

Fred was a whirlwind for the next several days. The Foundation was started, the auto shop had a nice big metal building. Everyone was smiling.

Only a few more things to do before everything comes together.

Fred called me and said that he was ready for his big performance. It was all set up with the principal players. I called one of my students and he made the call.

"Hello, 911, what is your emergency?" The dispatcher said.

"I just saw a known criminal on the street. It was that guy in the paper yesterday." He said.

"What is your name sir, and where are you?" The Dispatcher asked.

"I am Xavier Onassis, and I am at Four Hundred South and Main. He's the money guy. He's at the TRAX line." He said.

The police responded quickly. There was even a TV reporter with them. They captured him with guns drawn, handcuffed him, and hauled him away to jail in a Black Mariah. He was charged with a gun violation, counterfeiting and money laundering and remanded to jail.

The report that the TV gave was that he would be held in custody until his trial. Actually I took Fred out in disguise and under cover with Jim and Glenn Fields, the Foundation lawyer.

We will set him up in OUR BANK next week. Otherwise, he has not been seen since. Many of the USSS agents volunteered to be in the bank. I was surprised, they are all talking about it.

After the grand opening of the bank, Fred, with his disguise, had to appear in court. The judge asked him to go straight, and he said he would, now that he found a job. He made a point to say that he would be working in a bank, and told which one.

There were quite a few visitors in the courtroom during his hearing. Most of them I had never seen, but Jim and I took a lot of very quiet photos of them. I will run them through to get names and addresses. I hope I find some counterfeiters.

"I walked around in Building 403 showing the picture you gave me and asking if anyone had seen him. I got names of three people that he talked to. Here's the list." He said and handed me the list of names.

"Great work, Steve!" I said and he handed me a sheet of paper.

I asked him, "Do any of you know these named people?" I read the names off of the list.

One of the girls said she knew Ahmed Taylor. I got all the information written down here.

Emily has a copy of the University Annual, maybe we can find his picture in it.

Emily opened the book and leafed through it till she found him. Everyone crowded around to get a look. At least now we know one guy we need to find.

Chapter 16

The Foundation

Fred knew a lawyer, Glenn Fields, who could set up our Foundation in Utah. We made an appointment and hurried to his office for a nice long chat.

"I can establish the foundation for you, but we have a lot of work to do before we get this started. Filling out the Form 1023 takes a lot of time and patience, and I will need you to answer most of the questions. Where will you keep the money?" Glenn asked.

"We have a little bank building down on Fifteenth South that we will be using."

"You own a bank here?" Glenn was shocked at that revelation.

"No. I just closed one because of criminal operations going on there."

"We don't have any money in the bank yet, but we hope they will bring us some soon."

"You hope?" He said.

"We have to contact our unknown important depositors."

"I don't even want to know." He said and shook his head.

"You will have to establish a Board of Directors." He said. "Are you going to be the head of security?"

"Fred will do that and he will be the Bank President as well."

"That should be easy enough. The principals would be Mike, Ted, Jake, Lieutenant Ray, if he wants, and you and Fred. No one outside this group should know anything. My wife Denise will own everything, since she is invisible."

"We will want to draw up a plan of action before we do anything. This will tell what must be done and in what order. I will help you with this as well." Glenn said.

"Now we need to see a Financial Planner. I hope you have one in your back pocket. We can get this all wrapped and ready to sell to the crooks as soon as we get this complete."

Fred called a Financial Planner that he knew, Joseph Brooks. "Hey Joe, this is Fred. I would like to discuss a Foundation with you. We have an idea." He said.

We met Joseph at his office an hour later. Fred gave him all the details about the money and what we wanted to do with it.

"You won't want to put all the money into one mutual fund. It's always better to diversify, and I suggest that you hold some back in cash for little emergencies. Tell me again how much there is." Joe said.

"Nothing yet. We're waiting on it now." Fred said.

"What do you do with the Foundation?" Joe asked.

I explained our program of replacing old, worn out cars and trucks with newer restored ones.

"Wow! I like that. You could initially put all you want in a certain growth and income fund that I have been watching for some time. We could get things started and then spread any additional funds out in smaller bites, after you get established, to bond or gold funds." Joe said.

"We have done this before, I think this will go very well."

"You will have to do a lot of paperwork and you will need a Board of Directors, too." He said.

"You know that you will be on the Board of Directors, don't you?" I said with some amount of humor in my voice and a smile on my face.

"I was afraid of that but I'll help when I can." Joe said. "Keep the other money in a safe place."

It was a productive couple of days. We put the mutual fund together, all we need now is the money. I'm glad we hired a smart money man to handle the affairs of the Foundation.

Now that the money and the legal items are taken care of, we can have our first Board meeting. Denise has volunteered to be the secretary.

We have a video connection between Denise back home and our office in KC and in the bank president's office.

"What is Mike doing there? I don't mind Ted and Jake, but Mike brings a whole new brand of - - - well you know what I mean."

"Nice to see you too cousin. Does the new guy know what a crazy you are?" Mike said.

"Why, yes he does. We have had him out on a few adventures."

Denise called each Board member by name and position.

Glenn Fields, Legal, Joseph Brooks, Treasurer, Mike McCoy, Security, Ted Collins and Jake

Andrews, Cyber Security, Ron Windsor, Public Relations, Lieutenant Raymond Wright, Political Relations, and Fred Martin and David Wynn.

"Wait a minute! Doesn't this Wynn guy have a job here? Mike asked loudly.

"Why, no. I don't exist in this town. Thank you."

"Man! What a slacker!" He said.

They all laughed back home, but I feel sure that the guys in Salt Lake didn't understand any of it.

"By the way, folks, we are going to need some money out here. We have to get the auto shop going. Would you like to send it out, I could pick it up, or one of you could bring it. Whatever you decide is good with me."

"How much do you need?" Denise asked.

"A million should be plenty. I don't think we should need more than that here, but problems always jump up at us."

"First, we should pay off all the debts of the principals out of the fund like we did before. All payoffs must be anonymous, so they will be paid in cash delivered by a courier. That would be me. This way hackers can't get to us and there would be no way to blackmail someone."

"Second, we will hire a genius hacker to keep computer geeks from getting in. Don't forget, retaliation on the hacker geeks will be part of our plan. I'd say that Ted and Jake could do this, but they have other things to do. But this guy would work directly for Ted and Jake."

"The bank we closed had a lot of counterfeit and we're still going through it."

"We'll take care of it." Ted said.

"We checked all the other employees out and found them jobs elsewhere in town, and we kept two tellers here with us in the bank."

"Another thing. Could you have Ted send some software to help with the bank?" Maybe his Identity Thief software could go to terrorists or hackers and destroy all their software, too."

"It sounds like I should be the one to deliver the money. I could bring Jake and the software and get you started right. Besides, I've not been to Salt Lake before. Jake and I could be tourists for a couple days." Ted said.

"Sounds good to me. Just tell me the info on your flight and we'll have a parade just for you two."

Every day I check the classified ads in the local Paper. I thought by some miracle there might be a tow truck for sale. So far no luck. I put the word out to all the folks I work with, but still nothing.

"Hey David. Did you know there is a car auction here in town. Every Thursday over in Granite Park. Today's Thursday. You want to go?" Ray said.

"Sure! You drivin'?"

It was a short drive to the car auction. I was pumped. They might have just what we need. That would be great!

I registered and we ran in to the lot. Since a tow truck is higher than a normal car I jumped up in the bed of a pickup to get a better view.

"Over there!" I shouted and jumped down and hurried in the direction of what I saw. You wouldn't believe it. I didn't believe it. A 1953 Ford Tow Truck in blue and white with two million miles on it, a little rust, a few dents, and it started right up. The motor sounds good. I tried low and reverse gear and they moved it a foot or two. I let it warm up and shut it off. This is the one.

"I don't know what it's worth, but I'm going to bid on it."

"It's a '53, it can't be too expensive." Ray said.

When it was the tow truck's turn on the block, they towed it in. I must have run all the gas out of it, and no one knew it but me. The auctioneer started the bidding and I raised my hand to accept the first bid. Three or four guys were looking at it, but when the auction guys couldn't get it started, everyone quit. They all walked away and the auctioneer looked at me with a slight smile and said, "Sold!" I bought it for almost nothing.

Ray called his friend, Brad, at the car lot and told him to bring his tools, a can of gas and a tow truck driver. It didn't take long to get the paperwork on the tow truck in my hands. We will get the title changed tomorrow.

Fred and I sat and laughed for a few minutes about the tow truck with a glass of tea and I told him a few ideas that I had about the new building and what he would be doing.

"Mark said that he would deliver it this week." Fred said.

"I would pay the seller, or the guys on his crew, or your guys, a thousand extra to put it up for us. But they would have to be really quick about it." I said.

It took them a couple of days to find the building for Fred, but it looked perfect in the drawings Mark brought to Fred. I've seen these drawings before.

There are two big double doors in front, one on the right and one on the left with a walk door in the center that leads to the office and the main shop. He got it at a really big discount from a place that wasn't going out of business. They just wanted to unload it.

I paid for it and Fred and his crew put it together in less than a week and once the utilities are added, it will be a welcome addition to Brad's business.

Chapter 17

Finally, Woody

"I have always wanted a '40 Ford Woody Wagon. A real one. But they are extremely rare and hard to find."

I was just thinking out loud to myself when Ray said something that brought me out of my fantasy and back to reality.

"I know where there is one." He said

"What? Did I say that out loud? - — - You do?"

"He only has the wood part in the back of his barn. Maybe he has the rest of it too". He said.

I was so excited that I insisted we go see this guy immediately. Ray drove his truck out of town to a farm and we talked to, Pete, the farmer he knew.

"Sure, it's in the barn out here." Pete said.

We walked with him to his barn and way in the back of his barn covered by hay, dirt and a lot of other junk, was the wood body of some old Ford Woody Wagon.

"This is only the wood part. Do you have the rest of the metal car with the motor?"

"No, I sold that to Joe Jenkins several years ago." Pete said.

"Where does he live?"

"Up the road toward Bountiful. I'll draw you a map." He said.

Here we go again on the little two-lane and dirt roads on the way to another farm.

Joe Jenkins farm was easy to find and he was easy to talk to.

"Pete told us that you bought the body of a '40 Ford from him a few years ago. Do you still have it?" Ray said.

"Yeah! You know, I never did anything with that junker. Would you like to see it? I sure would like to get it out of my barn." Joe said.

Here we go again. We trekked out to his barn and moved a lot of things he had stored everywhere. And there it was! It looked like it had been put in against the back wall of his barn years ago and not looked at since then.

It was covered with everything you could imagine. It was all here waiting for us to uncover it. Joe finally got the hood up and there it was, a 1940 Ford flat-head V-8. The motor was still in it. All four tires were flat but the running gear was still in place.

"What would you like to give me for this thing?" He asked.

Ray threw out a number and he took it right then. I was surprised. It couldn't write the check fast enough.

"You'll have to move it yourself. I don't have any way to do it." He said.

"I hope you can help us get it out of the barn."

"Sure, I can do that. My boys will help." He said.

"Do you know anyone that might have a flatbed trailer that would hold it?"

"Yeah, I do. Bill Pace. He's down the road about a mile or two on the right." He said. "I'll get my boys to pull the car out while you're gone."

Here we go again. This time Lieutenant Ray is laughing all the way.

It was only a few minutes before we drove up the driveway that Joe told us about.

"Hi. Are you Bill Pace?" Ray said.

"Yes. How can I help you?" Bill said.

"We just bought an old car from your neighbor Joe. He said that you might have a trailer that we could buy and use to haul it away."

"Yeah, I have something behind that barn there." He said and pointed the way.

We all walked around and found it covered with hay and dirt, too. Everything is like that around here. It's a two axle wooden flatbed about twenty-five feet long. Two of the tires were flat, but he said he could get air in them if we wanted it. We settled on a very cheap price and hauled it away. I happily wrote another check.

In a few more minutes we were back to Joe's place hauling the old decrepit car out of his barn. Joe had a winch and we used it to pull the car up on the trailer. It was beautiful. I bought the winch too.

Here we go back to Pete's place, and the last stop I hope. Again it took all three of us to haul that old wood body out of his barn, even with the winch. The wood has a lot of age on it, but it didn't look like it was rotten.

We stuffed everything on the trailer and Pete and Ray had some rope and straps to tie it all down. I'm glad, because I don't want anything happening to this beauty. I'll buy some more straps when we get to town. Jim and I are going to haul all of this back to the Springs and present it to Norm. He'll know what to do with it. Then I have to drive back to Salt Lake and be ready for work by Monday. It's gonna be a long weekend.

I wrote three of the best checks I have ever written before. I bought a Ford Woody Wagon do-it yourself kit. What a deal!

"Do you know that the car is not a 1940?"

"No kidding? How do you know that? Ray said.

"Those two little oval grills at the bottom of the fenders near the hood. They were on the 1941 Ford."

"So what you have back there is a 1941 Ford Woody. Isn't that better?" Ray said.

"I guess it depends on how you look at it. But, it's OK with me. I'm as happy as I can be."

I had to get some rest if Jim and I were going to be able to drive to the Springs and back in only two days. I set my alarm for early in the morning and Jim was knocking on my door before I was dressed.

"You ready? Let's get going!" He said.

Jim and I spent fourteen hours driving back to the Springs with that trailer loaded with wood and metal. We went straight to Norm's shop and we were glad that there was still a light on when we pulled up. I stopped and Jim ran in. He got one of the big doors open and I pulled our big load inside.

Norm was there late doing books or paperwork. I didn't know he usually worked so late. Once we got it parked he began to laugh and make a few unseemly remarks which I ignored and Jim laughed.

"Hi guys. Looks like you have had a lot of fun in Salt Lake. Where did you dig this one up?" Norm said.

"I told you I was looking for one of these and I mentioned it at the Station there and someone said they knew where this was. I couldn't resist! It took us one whole day of running around to get it all on the trailer. Do you think there is a chance it will live again?"

"We'll inspect it very closely and I'll call you with a report." Norm said.

Play time is over! Now we go back to work!

Monday morning the classes began again. There is a lot more to talk about with money laundering. I spent the whole class time answering questions and explaining as best as I could how the whole system works.

"I still don't understand why the banks won't take the money and how they know it's bad money." Steve said.

I can see they are stuck on this one point. We'll have a lot more of these discussions. The bell rang and I told them that we will continue this at the next class.

"I think we should take a ride in the mountains and look for gold." Jim said.

"I think you're right. Let's go. We know there is someone up there, they shot at us. I'll have the IR with me this time."

I doubt that Finch is up there. I don't have any idea where he is. I wish I knew more about him.

We drove along all the back roads we could find, and checked each mine one by one. Each one was the same. The wood building, the mine cars sitting around, the tracks into the mine. But no people, and no evidence of people in the near past.

While we were at the fifth mine, I heard a gunshot and a bullet hit the wall of the building near me. I jumped behind a tree. I don't need another shock like the other day.

"Well, well. It looks like we have some fun coming our way."

There were only a couple guys hiding outside behind the mine cars. Jim went one way and I went the other. One guy stood up to take a shot at me and I surprised him.

"Physstt!"

When he went down, the other guy stood and Jim put him away.

"Physstt!"

I called 911 and reported what we had. The squad came later and filled lots of evidence bags and hauled the bodies away.

"Hey Ray, we never did hear who these guys are from up here. Have you got any ID on any of them yet?"

"So far they are just crooks hiding out from the law. None of them registered as counterfeiters or money men." Ray said.

Oh well, back to school tomorrow.

We delivered the woody to Norm weeks ago. Norm called today and had something he wanted us to know.

"DJ, this is Norm. You won't believe this but we found a package way back in the wood part of the car under a window and another tucked in behind the dash of the metal part of the car."

"Both packages contained thousands of dollars in old money dated from the time the car was new. I'm sending it to you to do with whatever you want. We don't feel like we should keep it, even though we found it." Norm said.

"I really appreciate what you did, Norm. I know exactly what to do with it. I'm going to give the money to the guys that we bought the cars from."

"By the way, was there anything special you wanted me to do to this monster?" He said.

"Only this. Paint it the original Ford Maroon of that time. But with better paint."

"Where did you get that three color car?" Norm asked.

"I bought it here in Salt Lake."

"What are you going to do with it when you come home?" He asked.

"I'll turn it over to the Foundation. It's a '62 Grand Prix. It should be nice when it's finished."

Mike called the next day and said that they had a nice trip to CU in Boulder.

"We found another corrupt professor in Boulder. Also a Colorado State Representative in Denver. They were working together. They had influenced several students with their evil messages. I hope we can straighten out the students. They're all in jail now."

I was notified that a break in the counterfeit case might fall in our lap this week.

Someone in Flagstaff tipped off one of our guys that a big load of paper would be going north. We managed to get one of our men in as the assistant driver into the truck. The load would be over a thousand pounds. The biggest thing we didn't know was what the destination was to be. Jim and I in our old Grand Prix and Ray and his partner in a non-descript Japanese minivan did a tag team follow on the truck.

We picked up the truck south of Provo on US-89. I began to hear someone talking. I didn't recognize the voice. When I spoke I got a response through my ear bud. I don't understand, but I'm going to try to find the speaker.

"Hi."

"U SS?" The voice said.

"SS." I said.

"Good. Listen." The voice said again.

"K!"

"It's either the driver or the assistant driver." I told Jim.

"Coming to SLC." He said.

"Yeh."

"Need gas." He said.

The truck pulled into the next gas station on the highway. We pulled into one of the other pumps. The passenger got out and began filling the tank and the driver went to the building to pay the bill. I followed and as the driver turned around I said. "Three color car."

"K." He said.

They changed positions at the gas station. Now our guy was the passenger.

I told Jim and he went back to tell Ray.

"I've been listening." Ray said.

When the truck entered Salt Lake, it didn't stop. It just kept going up I-80 toward Cheyenne. Just past Rockport it turned off and made a turn toward Coalville. We couldn't follow too close because the truck driver would see the dust.

The assistant driver had the ear bud and he was speaking the turns as they happened. Ray and I stopped and waited for the truck to stop. But, by that time they were out of range and we lost the signal. Ray hit the gas and we were off again. It took another mile or so before we regained the signal and our guy said they were stopping and read the name on the old gold mine.

Jim had his camera with him at the ready. The audio recorder had been running since the beginning. The driver met two men and they opened the back doors of the truck. There were pallets with huge boxes tied to them.

We heard a voice say something about getting it all unloaded so they could get out of there. There was a little forklift in the mine and it took the pallets and put them into the mine behind one of the old mine cars.

The driver and our assistant driver got in the truck and sped away.

Ray and his partner and Jim and I walked up to the two guys at the mouth of the mine.

"Hi guys. Whatcha got in the boxes?" Ray asked.

"Nothin' you'd want to see." One said.

"My friends and I always like to see new stuff." Ray pulled out his badge and showed it to them.

"You can't look at anything here. You need a Search Warrant for that, and you'd have to say what you're looking for." He said.

"Whatever makes you think that? Those boxes are out here in plain sight." Ray said. "Just so you know, we know there's a load of paper in those boxes. I'd just like to see it."

The other one made a small move toward his jacket pocket and I pulled out James Bond and waved it at him. He dropped his hand and stood there without any more movement.

"You probably better give that to me. I don't want to shoot you to get it."

He pulled it out with two fingers and gently handed it to me. Why do they always carry a forty-five? I stuck it in an evidence bag and threw it in the trunk.

Jim and I went to our car and pulled out a hammer and a crowbar and pulled the top of one box open.

"Whaddaya know! It's full of money. You guys sure are lucky! I wish I had this much money delivered to me."

Ray's partner was already on the phone to the station. By the time the PD arrived at the mine, we had the two in handcuffs and their guns were in a plastic bag.

The squad officers got everything loaded up and carried away and the four of us were left standing there. One of us began to laugh and we all caught it. We finally got settled down and decided to get back to Sanityville.

If you get around the crazies and stay with them for too long, it rubs off. I don't want any of that on me.

Our guy, the assistant driver was revealed to the PD once they were alone in one of the offices. He will be charged and arrested the same as the driver, but our guy will be released and not seen again by any of the Flagstaff people.

Now we have a big handle on the counterfeiting here.

Chapter 18

Money And Software

The FBI ran the prints and pictures from the University Annual book. They found one teacher as a terrorist, the other two are just crooks. All three have been removed from the school.

Ted and Jake arrived by commercial air in the morning. Jim and I were there to meet them with our three color car. They both had something to say about it. We loaded their luggage and took them to the Rodeway to check in.

It was a busy day. The first thing to do was take the money to the new OUR BANK. We took the Cashier's Check to the Federal Reserve Bank and they said that they would deliver the cash to our bank as soon as the check cleared. That should be tomorrow.

Ted and Jake walked around the OUR BANK bank and gave it a thorough inspection. He was surprised when I told him the amount of counterfeit we found in the vault.

"We're still checking every bill in there. We're wrapping and banding all of it so it won't contaminate any of the good stuff."

"I've got the Identity Theft software that you can start installing in all the banks. That should help." He said.

"Let's leave that for the morning. Now we'll drive around this city and look at all the most interesting things they have here. You two are tourists now."

I drove the three color car all through the city and pointed out some of the most interesting places there. The Temple, the Tabernacle and the State Capitol Building are all together in the center of town. When they found out that the Tabernacle Choir rehearses on Thursday night, they immediately said that they wanted to see that.

From there we went through the University of Utah and Fort Douglas. Then the Salt Palace and ended the tour at Trolley Square. They enjoyed it a lot. They commented at every stop. I'll bet that Ted will want to bring his family here for a vacation sometime.

We spent all morning driving around Salt Lake and seeing the sights, but now it's time to get something happening. I introduced Ted and Jake to Lieutenant Ray and his squad. Ted began his talk with the ID software and Jim and I slipped out the back door.

We have been in Salt Lake for several months now and we have found a few of the places where the druggies hide. It's time we took a few of them out and sent a message that things have changed in town.

It didn't take long to attract their attention.

"Who are you and what are you doing on our street?" Someone said.

He was leaning on the side of a building trying to look like he was important and cool. He had a bag of white powder in one hand and the other hand was in a pants pocket. I assumed it was handling a pistol. A small pistol judging from the bulge in the pocket.

"We were looking for some drug dealers to tell that we have taken over the business in this town, and that they should all leave before we take them out."

He started to pull the pistol, but he was paying attention to the wrong guy. Jim already had James Bond out and leveled on him.

"Physstt!"

"You should have answered me!" I said to him as he melted onto the sidewalk.

Jim called Ray and I looked for any other candidates. None appeared.

When we returned to the station, I looked up Ted and told him what we were going to do.

"You guys need to get a rental car. Jim and I are going fishing."

We took them to the car rental at the airport and waited while they rented one. It didn't take long.

"Be careful, those guys might be able to shoot straighter than the ones you've seen before." Ted said.

We found what looked like the Store Front gang that we cleaned out back in KC. This group wasn't any smarter.

"Physstt!" "Physstt!" "Physstt!" "Physstt!" "Physstt!"

We had to look for the leader for a few days, but he's now resting with his gang.

Jim said that he had heard there was a new drug dealing outfit in town and he thought it was time to hunt them down for ourselves. Jim got a tip a few days ago that this new bunch was in West Jordan.

West Jordan is south of Murray and on the other side of the interstate. We drove slowly through the back streets and alleys. I thought it would be easy to find them with our three color car and old clothes.

Jim parked and we walked around the block. Finally we were set upon by two young guys in their twenties. One of them had a handful of little bags. The other had a pistol. Now we're talking!

"You guys lookin' for some fun?" The one with the bags said.

"Yeah! Whatcha got?" Jim asked.

"We got everything! Cocaine, crack, sugar, anything you want." He said.

"What we really want is the guy with some money. You know, the big money."

"Oh yeah! You mean Jackson. Two blocks down in the brick warehouse on the left. But you better have an invitation. He don't let everybody in." He said.

"He'll let me in. I'm One Shot McCoy from KC."

"Oh!" He said.

"I guess my reputation has spread all the way out here. Good!"

It didn't take long to find Jackson's building. We parked and entered the front door and were greeted by two big fellas with guns.

"Who are you and what are you doing here?" One said.

"I'm One Shot McCoy and this is my partner, Jim. I came to see Jackson about his money."

He pulled out his phone and started talking. I could tell that the person on the other end was asking some tough questions. He would stop and look at me then say something, then look at Jim.

"He wants to know what kind of weapon that you carry." He said.

I opened my jacket so he could see James Bond.

"It's a little nine mil with a silencer in a shoulder holster." He said. "Yes sir, right away."

"You can go up now. Those stairs." He said and pointed the way for us.

Jim and I took the stairs to the second floor and two more guys stopped us for another look. They took us to the man's office and even opened the door for us.

He was sitting at a large very impressive desk with two guys sitting along the wall to his right and left.

"So you're One Shot McCoy?" Jackson said.

I walked to his desk and extended my hand to him. We shook hands and I sat directly in front of him, Jim was next to me.

"What can I do for you today?" He asked.

"I came to make you an offer. I understand the money business. I also understand that you need a place to deposit that money where no one will see or touch it. I have such a place. We recently came into a deal where I acquired the bank on Fifteenth South."

"That was you?" He said with a surprised voice.

"Yes, it was. I have brought in my own people to run it now. We will still cater to the public, but we can handle all that you might want to store in our safe deposit boxes. But we won't take counterfeit. I don't like to get involved with it"

"OK. No counterfeit. I'm good with that. One more thing, could you show me this "James Bond' that Mike McCoy has mentioned?" He asked.

"Sure." I pulled open my jacket and let him see it.

"You carry that all the time?" He asked.

"Every day, all day long. This is James Bond."

"You any good with it?" He asked.

"I am called One Shot for a reason."

"There was a guy in KC that brought the laundry together there." He said.

"You mean Perry? I haven't seen him for a long time. Maybe someone got him."

"Where is he? He asked.

"No one knows. We have all searched for him for months, but no luck."

"What about his artist?" He asked.

"Sawbuck was in a bad auto accident and the cops found him in a hospital. He's in jail now."

"If you want to use OUR BANK, why don't you come up and look it over? I'll give you a tour myself."

"OK. I'll bring a couple of my boys and we'll see what we can do." He said.

After we left Jackson's building I said to Jim. "I think we put his mind at ease with the talk about Perry and Sawbuck."

I had asked Ted to bring the Identity Theft software with him and he did. He is briefing the PD unit what it does and how it does it. We all will be distributing the new program throughout the metro area to each and every bank and credit union.

Their cyber specialists made copies of the program for each two-man team to take to the businesses around the city.

Jackson and two of his boys showed up on Thursday of the next week. I took all three of them around so that my people could see them, get fingerprints, photos and DNA if possible to send to the FBI for identification.

"I will need to know what your guys will be wearing. I wouldn't want to talk to the wrong people. Do you have some kind of a uniform that they could wear during the deliveries?"

"Yes, we can do that." He said. "I have a laundry truck at the office. There will be dressed in white or light blue coveralls, and they will wear 'Beehive Laundry' work clothes."

"Be sure they have name tags." Just then Fred walked up to us. "Well, here is my new Bank President, Mister Grant."

I introduced Fred to Jackson and his two guards.

"What's this going to cost me?" He asked.

"One percent per month. Cheap at twice the price."

Fred and Jackson shook hands and Jackson said. "This looks like what we need to get things sorted out."

"One more thing. No more than two suitcases full per day and no more than two deliveries each week. It wouldn't look right if the people saw you here too often."

Jackson seemed pleased with our arrangement. He took the two bodyguards and left.

Ted spent all day explaining about how his software program works and how it will help find Identity Thieves and terrorists if they use the computer to contact people. The anti hacker part fascinated most of them.

Ted took some of them out to a bank close by and actually showed the how to do the install and how it will show up on their computer screens.

Jim and I walked in a few minutes after Ted and Jake had finished their lecture. They will start installing the Identity Thief software in the banks tomorrow.

Every day my class asks what we have been doing since the previous class. For some reason they think what I do is fun and exciting. I have a brilliant idea.

"Say Ray. How would you like to have some help with the banks? I have a whole classroom full of kids who want to get involved with the 'crime fighting' business."

"How old are they?" He asked.

"College kids. Why don't you drop in on my class tomorrow and you can see for yourself?"

"OK. I will." He said.

I introduced Lieutenant Ray to the class and told what he would be doing.

"I have received great help from the Police force, and now you people are going to have a chance to help them. Two man teams will be going to each of the banks in town and installing a program that defends against thieves and terrorists. You can be part of that team."

I hadn't finished talking before some of them were walking to the front of the classroom. They were ready to go. They piled into their cars and were off.

Jackson didn't waste any time getting the first deposit delivered to OUR BANK. Two guys appeared just after lunch with two suitcases full of that wonderful green stuff. I got a couple of the girls to take it into the vault and empty the suitcases into some deposit boxes.

Now the girls will really start working.

It took a few more days to get all the special equipment bought and delivered to OUR BANK.

We set up something in the basement like we did in KC and the Springs. All the various machines needed to identify counterfeit, count the money, record the serial numbers, and trace the money to the various jobs and victims was now installed and working in our special room in the basement.

Chapter 19

Music On Thursday

We finally got the report from the FBI on the fingerprints and handwriting analysis on the mysterious notebooks found in the bottom of an old unused school locker. He was in school during the time that our three enemy agents were in school also. The person's name was Arnold Gilmore.

Arnold finished his college degree and secured a job with the Federal Government as a legal clerk for a Congressman in Washington, D.C. Arnold later ran for a Senate seat from Colorado and was elected.

When Arnold became a Senator, he concentrated on finding and removing the Professor and the kids the professor had been teaching at the college and putting them in jail. The professor had several kids at the time on their way to being a great threat to our state and country.

Arnold was responsible for the apprehension of all of the young agents, they weren't so young at the time he jailed them. But he could not stop the Professor from getting away. It was only a year or so later that Arnold died in an automobile accident. It all looks fishy. It looks like the Professor or Downey killed Arnold.

Mike sent me a photo of the Professor that was with some personal effects of Arnold. He tried to get the professor for terrorism and treason.

"Hey! I know this guy! Isn't this Finch?" Jim said.

"So Finch is the professor from Colorado. Whaddaya know? The one I shot was named Downey, so he wasn't in that first group. I wonder how many there are."

"We need to get this creep and put him away!" Jim said.

"We will continue to hunt for this low life until we find him."

I called Jackson and told him that half of the paper he brought in was phony. He went through the roof. He came to the bank right away. Then he wanted to see it for himself. I took him into the President's office and ran a handful of bills through the machine. Every one of them showed up as counterfeit.

"Someone has been substituting funny money for the stuff they owe me! I've got work to do!" He said. And he was gone.

We know that Jackson is in the Laundering business, but he's not the head man. Since there is not a casino in the state, he won't be going that direction unless they take it to Nevada or Colorado. Both are too far to risk the trip.

I have been trying to get the class to meld into the law enforcement mold without actually being in dangerous situations. If they are so gung-ho about this I have to be careful about what they are really thinking and doing.

"I have an assignment for you. We found the Travelling Terrorist had made a stop in building 403. We were told that he spoke to Ahmed Taylor and two other students. We need to know who those students are. We also need to find them and Ahmed. Can you do it?"

Three of them stood up and said they would get on it now and they left the classroom.

We all agreed that we should put a tail on Ahmed Taylor. We must have the tail call at every stop he makes and identify any people that Ahmed talks to. Names and photos would be good. The traveling terrorist talked to three people in 403. Ahmed was one of them. We need to know who the other two are.

No one has seen Ahmed, is he a crook? What if he is dead?..Who are the other two?

"Now another assignment for some of you. Has anyone found the address or the people who live in the white house with the name Elliot in Park city?"

"Yes, I have it right here. One of the boys stood up and handed me a paper with all the news."

"Did they check out?"

"We couldn't find anything bad in their background." He said.

"OK. We'll cross them off. I wonder why he stopped there." - - - - "Maybe it was one of the houses next door that he was going to. Could you clear that up for me?"

"We'll get right on it." He said.

"Jim and I will check out the Fort. We have some connections there."

The driver and our assistant driver were taken to the station and each put in a different room. Our Foundation lawyer and I got the assistant out of there without being seen. I took him to the airport and he boarded a flight out of town.

After the driver answered a battery of questions they found that his company received a call to pick up a load at a warehouse. The directions were given over the phone and payment was waiting stapled to the top of one of the wooden crates.

The address and directions to where the crates were to be delivered were also stapled to the crates. There were no charges brought against the driver, but his help was enlisted to find the source of the delivery.

Our truck driver picked up the load of counterfeit in Flagstaff. We alerted all the agents and law enforcement in the area, but nothing so far.

The two guys in the mine with the counterfeit sang like canaries, but they really didn't know very much. They gave us some names in the local Salt Lake area, but they were small timers, not the bosses.

We'll keep on it and we will clean them out of town. One way or another.

The prints and photos we sent to FBI for identification ID's came back. Two names showed up that had history in Counterfeiting and Money Laundering. Now we must put faces on them and find them. This is good! We have some interest.

A few days later our guys in Flagstaff called Ray and told him that they shut down and removed the printing plant for the counterfeit and cleaned out the warehouse. There was millions of dollars worth of twenties, fifties and hundreds stored in boxes all around the rooms.

Now we must find the people in the Salt Lake area who are the distributors.

Bright and early Thursday morning I got a call from Ted.

"Since today is Thursday, do you think we can get in to see the Tabernacle Choir do their rehearsal? Jake and I have been waiting all week for this."

"You bet. It is a priority!" It starts at seven, you will want to be early. There might not be any seats for you."

Later in the day, Norm called me from the Springs.

"I just wanted to put your mind at ease. I think I can get the Woody running. We have taken the motor, transmission and rear end completely apart and dug all the dirt and grease out of them. I don't have them put back together yet, but we're working on it." Norm said. "We haven't started on the wood yet. That will come much later."

"Thanks Norm, I really appreciate all your extra hard work for me."

Jim and I worked on all kinds of paperwork for the rest of the day. Jim wanted to go to someplace different for lunch, so Ray took us all to a new place across the street from the Farmer's Market. Ted has always been an aficionado of food and he really heaped the praise on this place.

The time to go to hear the music must be here. Ted and Jake are standing next to our desks and making funny sounds like you do when you're in a hurry.

We all rode in Ted's car. I didn't want anyone seeing the three color car at the Tabernacle. I took them up to the nosebleed section so they could have a better overall view of the choir. They loved it! I haven't seen Ted this excited before since he got married.

They wanted to get a bite after we were outside, so I took them to the Rio Grande Café in the train station. Naturally we had to see the Zephyr come in. We all jumped on and rode it while the train was turned on the wye. That brought a lot of smiles to all of our faces. Sometimes you need a smile.

Chapter 20

Fishing

We drove up and down every little dirty dusty road and path looking for the professor. We went to every little town starting at the bottom of the hill and working up. Debbie said she saw Finch in the car with another guy. She didn't know who the other guy was and neither do we. But she finally said that she wasn't sure which road it was.

We searched records at the courthouse of Salt Lake, Rich, Summit and Wasatch Counties for any clue about the professor and his hideout. There were a few Finches here and there, but not the one we wanted.

I know he's here. We are going to go to every little town and research the books in their courthouse. There are so many dirt roads out here that the three color car is getting washed more times than I am.

Of the four counties in the Salt Lake area, we already finished Salt Lake County. I think Rich and Summit County is a stretch. That leaves Wasatch County as our first stop.

Jim and I drove to the courthouse in Heber. It took us a little time to explain what we wanted to the various clerks until we got to the Mayor. He took us to a clerk and told her what we wanted and to help all she could.

Now all we had to do was plow through each and every tax record on each and every house and apartment in the town. Simple!

I only have a week left before the semester begins again, so we really got after it. Everything was in alphabetical order. Jim and I would each take a page and work through it. I'm reading the names of the owners and tenants if they are available.

Every time I read a name that sounds familiar it stops me, but it only takes a second to think about it. They like the names of country singers, so that's really what I'm looking for here. Now if it was obvious like Waylon Jennings, I would get excited, but that's not the way it is going.

I know it won't be a woman's name and I don't think this professor is smart enough to use the newer batch of singers. So I'm looking for names from the fifties to the seventies.

We've been here all day and I have only plowed through to the G's. I'll be back tomorrow to start there. We notified the Mayor and he has agreed to help as long as he can.

I called Luigi Puzo in Albuquerque and asked him about their laundry operation in this area.

"We don't do much in Utah. They don't have any casinos in the state and we pretty much are hands off there." He said.

"Do you know a man named Jackson?"

"No. Can't say as I do. He's not one of ours." He said.

"He is the main man in it here that I have found. He may not be the boss, but he has some power. You might want to talk to him. What I really want to know is this. Are there any others working here and who are they."

"Where would I find him? I could send a few guys up there to get the information." He said.

I gave him all the details about the building and the two guys at the door, the two guys on the second floor and the two guys in Jackson's office. He said he would send someone up to ask a few questions.

"While you're at it, could you try to find out who is distributing the large amount of counterfeit in this area?"

"I'll make a point of it!" He said.

The next day Jim and I were in Heber again. We were plowing through the books when I found George Jones. That was the name they used back in the Springs when we were looking for Wilson and his crew.

"Hey Jim! Look at this!"

Jim came over and read the name that I pointed out to him.

"You don't think it could possibly be that easy, do you?" He said.

"Boy, I hope so. I'm really tired of going through these books. How would you like to do this for your regular job every day?"

"We better show this to Ray before we go charging off into the unknown." He said.

I walked into the interrogation room to find the bank president from Fifteenth South sitting at the table. He looked a little dejected. Wait till I'm done with him! He'll really feel bad!

"Well, look who's here. You are on the list of people that we don't like very well. I suppose you thought that the name you gave us would be your ticket out of this mess. Don't you know that every man in this country over the age of twenty knows who Bill Russell is?"

"You will have to do better than that this time. If you screw with me, I will shoot you. You can put that in the bank. I have a long history."

"This is the way it is going to work. I will ask you for the name, address and phone number of everyone involved in the counterfeit business in this town, or you will be in one of the metal boxes in that room in the basement."

"Maybe I should explain who I am before we start. I am the money police. I work for the people who actually print all the money in this country. There are three types of criminals who are rated the very worst in this country. Thieves, traitors and terrorists. So far you are on two of the three lists. Since counterfeit money is stealing real money from someone and giving them a worthless piece of paper, you are a thief. Since counterfeit money is degrading the economic system of this country, you are a traitor."

"I haven't found a way to include you into the terrorist group, but give me time."

"I have had all the lights out in the halls turned off. I wouldn't want anyone seeing what I might do to you. Now then, in front of you is a legal size tablet and more than one pen. You should take the pen and write down every name, address, phone number and fact that you know about counterfeiting that you can about all the counterfeiters in the state. I will wait!"

I think he got the message. He began to write and continued for about fifteen or twenty minutes.

I absent-mindedly let my jacket fall open more than once so that he could see James Bond.

Chapter 21

Hunting

I have been hunting for a canary that would tell me what I wanted to know. I think I might have found one.

"So you're the scumbag that beat up my friend. I don't like scumbags. I especially don't like the ones that sneak up on a guy and hit him in the head from behind. You fit all the categories that I don't like. What do you think I should do about that?

"Nothing you can do." He said with a smile.

"Why do you think that?"

"You're not a cop." He is still smiling.

"You're right. And they don't even know that I'm in here. I could whip your ass and walk out of here and you'd be laying on the floor and no one would even know how it happened. And the best part is this. If you told them, they wouldn't believe you. You do know who I am don't you?"

"You think you can whip me? I'm a lot bigger than you are." He said.

"When I was in second grade a kid from the seventh grade beat me and my friend up. But since then I learned Karate and seven other different ways to maim and kill a person."

"My favorite one of all of them is this." I opened my jacket and showed him James Bond. They call me One Shot. That's because if I get one shot, you're dead. Try me if you think you can."

He jumped up and I smacked his with James Bond's leg and he sat down with a slight trickle of blood on the side if his face. The smile has left him and now he doesn't know whether he should be angry or try to jump me again. I might shoot him. I might even like it. Actually, I'm sure that I would like it!

"Now then! I'm going to ask you some very easy questions, and if you tell me the truth, everything will go just fine for you. But if you lie to me or refuse to answer, I will shoot you in the thigh. My favorite spot."

"First question.' He expected a really hard one. He also didn't know that I knew what he would say. And that I would enjoy it.

"Where were you born." This is gonna be fun.

"Danbury, Connecticut." He said with a huge smile.

"Physstt!"

I smiled back at him and said. "Strike one!"

"OK! OK! Ryadh." He said.

"Well! Whaddaya know! That's in Saudi Arabia. How did you get into this country?" He is still yelling at the top of his lungs, but he knows now that he had better answer the questions, or else.

"The Professor did the paperwork and sent it in for me. I only signed what he told me to do." He said.

"Who is this professor?"

"Some guy that came to our school back home. I didn't want to live there and they sent me here to stay with him. He taught me everything." He said.

"Did he teach you how to kill people?"

"He said that the people in this country hate Allah and our people and that we should be careful of them and kill them if they threaten us." He said.

Has anyone threatened you?"

"No." He said.

I am going to hold this guy for a while and get a lot more information from him later. But now I have a more pressing job waiting.

It took us a long time to ferret out the counterfeiters, but with the help of One Shot McCoy and his friends in high places, we found and eliminated them.

I got a call from Luigi Puzo.

"Just thought I'd let you know that we found about a dozen guys in the funny money business. They all decided to leave town. Some went out feet first, but they went. None of them were ours. Nice doing business with you One Shot. See you soon." He said.

They may not have found them all, but the ones we missed should know that their life isn't worth much now. The wrong people are looking for them. If they are found with any funny money, both will disappear.

We know that George Jones lives, or at least, pays taxes in Heber. The address was smudged too badly on the page that we couldn't get the address. Ray and his partner have agreed to help us hunt for our wayward professor.

Up one street and down another. Two of us on one side and the other two on the other side. We started at the courthouse with maps and tablets. I would write the name of the street and Jim and I would walk it recording the house numbers.

I've had more fun that this in a dentist's office.

We had been at this for a couple of hours when Ray's phone rang and the PD needed him right away. Ray and his partner left and Jim and I continued for another hour until we got so tired we had to give it up for the day.

Jim and I were exhausted. We went back to the motel and took a nap. I woke up with Jim knocking at the door.

"You gonna sleep all day. I'm starting to get hungry and you have the car keys."

"Gimme a minute and I'll be ready. I didn't mean to sleep that long. What time is it?"

He held his arm up for me to see his watch.

"Man! I guess I was more tired than I thought. Here you drive. Pick any place you want to eat."

We stopped at a place that had the best Mexican food I have had in years and, of course, both of us ate too much.

Tomorrow we'll be back at in Heber.

Ray and his partner joined Jim and I the next morning to prepare for another grueling day of door-to-door hunting called 'police work'.

During the third block we were in, Ray yelled at us.

"Hey! I think I found him!" He said.

Ray was standing on the sidewalk and looking at a mailbox. It has the name 'Jones' on it.

Jim and I ran across the street to where Ray was standing. All four of us looked at the name on the mailbox.

"I don't believe it!"

"Right here out in the open! Jim said.

"Are you guys ready? I don't know what we might find inside." Ray said.

"OK! Let's go!

Chapter 22

One Last Shot

Debbie said she saw Finch in a car with a guy driving up the hill toward Park City. We searched for months all the roads all along the way. I might have missed it, but the name on the tax roll for this house was George Jones.

We finally found him in a house in Heber. Heber is a smaller town several miles from Park City, but it is the county seat. Jim and I and Ray and his partner went around the house to the back door, and entered as quietly as we could. Finch was sitting in a chair dozing when we entered the living room.

He must have heard us and he jerked to his feet and pulled a gun. I had always wanted to shoot this guy, I even had daydreams about it, and put him out of our misery, but I held up. I took careful aim and put one in his thigh.

"Physstt!"

He screamed and fell on the floor. I enjoyed that a lot.

"I don't usually shoot them in the thigh unless I want them to talk. But this guy has done so many bad and terrible things that I thought he needed to feel some of the pain he has spread around our country." I said to him.

I was talking more to myself than to anyone else. I was enjoying his screaming a lot. He gave me a very bad look and I smiled at him. He was still holding the gun, but he didn't quite know what to do with it.

"So this is the famous Professor James Finch. He matches the photo in the University Annual that Debbie showed us. He must be seventy five years old or more. That makes him a prime candidate for the role of the Professor from Colorado that we have been hunting for a very long time."

"Gee professor, I'm sorry I missed your heart, but if you don't talk to us, I'm sure I can try again. Do you remember a few people that I know? Congressman Wilson, a man named Downey and a Kansas State Representative named Hardesty?"

He was very obstinate, and made rude signs and noises like he didn't want to cooperate. He has been in this country long enough to understand the one finger salute. He screamed and crawled back onto the chair and got the gun onto his lap. I know he wanted to shoot me, but he was hurting so bad that he just couldn't make it.

"If you decide not to talk to us, you could end up like Downey. He found his rest in a morgue in Washington DC. But if you decide to cooperate with this nice man here, you might live long enough to visit my friends, and a couple of yours, in a little town in Kansas called Leavenworth."

"I don't usually shoot someone in the thigh unless I want them to talk to us, but since you already have a slug in your leg, you should start talking. You might as well tell Ray here what he wants to know or

I might get angry. And you wouldn't want to see me when I'm angry."

He finally got the message and began to talk to Ray. Once Ray had recorded all the discussion and screaming, he called 911 and had them send some folks, an ambulance and his squad, up the hill to pick him up. That leg will hurt him for a very long time. Maybe it will make him think of better things, but I doubt it.

Then the crap began to come out of him.

"You Americans are so stupid. I am so much smarter than you. I have degrees in many disciplines and you have none." He said. "Blah, Blah, Blah." He just kept going with his 'I'm better than you' routine. Meanwhile, he waved the gun around, but couldn't zero in on me.

This baloney went on for fifteen or twenty minutes. Ray looked at me with a quizzical look and Jim just sat down in one of the chairs.

He finally got his gun mostly stable and was swinging it around to face me.

One question kept flooding my mind.

Why am I even bothering with this guy? He has been instrumental in killing and injuring thousands of people in our country and others across the world. Let's just finish with him. After all, I am called One Shot McCoy!

I raised James Bond and squeezed.

"Physstt!"

Suddenly there appeared a round spot in the middle of his forehead and he dropped the pistol.

He crumbled to the floor like an old sack of trash ready to be carried out to the garbage can.

We didn't move him or touch anything until the guys with the ambulance came and put him in the back of the truck. There was a nurse and a doctor with them.

The professor was pronounced dead and the ambulance drove back to town.

Finally!

The next day Jim and I took a trip through the Fort where the Travelling Terrorist was reported to have stopped. This kind of thing is one of the hardest of all. Trying to find someone who might be on the wrong side without alerting them or panicking everyone in the neighborhood.

I'm going to turn this one over to Ray and his crew. I don't have any good hard evidence on anyone at the Fort. I also don't have any help there.

Chapter 23

Goodbye

It's almost the end of the semester and I will have to say goodbye to all the students in the class and the Salt Lake PD before we leave.

All the students wanted to know how to contact me.

"We still don't know who you really work for." Emily said.

"Just think about it. You are all smarter than you think. You have proved that every day we have been together. It will come to you. You're pretty smart. You will figure it out."

"That time that you said you fell and hurt your shoulder. You didn't really fall, did you? Somebody shot you didn't they?" Adam asked.

"Yes I had to admit that was what happened. He took me by surprise."

"Why were you not hurt more than you were?" Jean asked.

I opened my jacket and showed them the vest. They have already seen James Bond before this.

"Why are you wearing that now?" Joseph asked.

"In my business, you never know when a call might come in that would put you in danger, like the Firehouse. You don't have time to go home and find your vest."

"I have enjoyed this class. I hope you got something good out of it. You all have received a grade of 'A' for the course. If you are going to continue in any of this business, you will need more classes, and I hope they will be easier for you. Goodbye."

It's time for Jim and I to climb into our big blue plane and fly away, fly away.

Jim and I will be relieved to get home to our families and loved ones. I have been straining to see Denise, Mel and Jen especially. We've been through a lot together. I will still work with Norm and the Foundation. I enjoy giving money and cars away.

Jim and I made a special trip to see Fred at the bank.

"We caught all the counterfeiters in the area. I'm sure the vacuum will be filled soon, so be on your toes. We also found out that Jackson and his gang, seem to be missing. All that money he deposited in your bank is now the property of the bank. You should have about ten million, I think. You could use it for the Foundation or to help some destitute people. Your choice." I told Fred.

"I thought I would say goodbye to Brad at the car repair shop. You want to go with us?"

The three of us drove to the Auto Shop and gave Brad and Fred all the contact information on us and the Foundation.

We took Fred back to the bank and reported in to Lieutenant Ray and his people. I wanted to thank each and every one for all their help in this last project.

One last thing to do was to stop in at the Fort and say goodbye to Paul. We have been using a parking space near where Paul's unit is housed. It's reasonably close and it has the look of a little knoll beside it. Most everybody calls it the grassy knoll. I don't like that name since it brings death into the discussion. I just call it a hill.

I don't like death. It is a fact of life, but it doesn't need to be on our mind and in our thoughts daily. Yes, I remember the significance of the words. But that was not here.

I parked in our usual spot and Jim jumped out and turned to close his door when gunshots from behind me were heard.

"BANG!" "BANG!" "BANG!"

There's someone up the hill on the knoll shooting at us. I was out of the car with my back to the shooter. A bullet hit the car near the window to my right and went into the back seat.

Jim pulled his gun and emptied the clip where he saw the flashes.

"Physstt!" "Physstt!" "Physstt!" "Physstt!" "Physstt!"

I spun around ready to fire, but the firing had stopped. Jim and I slowly crept up the little hill and found two guys on the ground at the top. Jim is really good with that little pistol when he has to be.

It looks like we have to visit Lieutenant Ray again. I made the call and they were here in just a few minutes. Maybe these two were the ones that the

Traveling Terrorist stopped at the Fort to see that day. I hope.

The last thing of the day today was to check with the maintenance people at the airport. I wanted them to give our blue plane a good look before we fly out tomorrow. We have one more day of finish up work to do, and the next morning it's 'Up, Up and Away'.

Chapter 24

Back Home Again

I called Denise to tell her that we would be returning home tomorrow. She was overjoyed. She couldn't stop saying 'I'm so glad'. I gave her all the details of the flight, and told her to hug and kiss all the kids for me.

"The flight should take about three and a half hours. We plan to leave at ten o'clock in the morning. Could you pick us up at the Falcon airport?"

"I would be glad to pick you up, honey. See you then." She said.

When we finally returned home from Salt Lake, I wanted to get home and crash on the couch. Denise must not have been listening to me when I said it. Well I guess I was just thinking it, not speaking it.

Denise spent five minutes hugging and kissing me. That was the first time since we brought the old do-it-yourself car kit back home. I liked it a lot, but Jim was fidgeting, so we all piled into the car and were off.

Wait! Denise made a wrong turn. We should be going north toward our house. We are going west toward town. Wait a minute, this is Platte, and we're heading toward town. I commented and she said that we had to make a stop to see Norm. He must have missed our daily visits that Jim and I did. When we walked in he came hurrying over to us.

"Man, am I ever glad to see you two. We have been busy and we turned out a lot of cars for the people. I have a Letter and a Plaque from the City for the Foundation. It seems that many of the recipients of the cars called and wrote the Mayor about what a great thing we did for them." Norm said.

"Hey! While you're here, I want you to see something special." He said.

We walked all the way to the back wall and right to the farthest corner. There was a lump with a huge cover over it.

"Come on. Give me a hand with this you guys." He said.

Jim and I pulled on the cover and it finally came off of the lump. It's the Woody!

"Wow! It's the Woody!" I was talking very loud and didn't realize it. It took me a few minutes to get myself settled down to normal.

"The Woody that we brought back from Salt Lake! Wow! It is beautiful!"

I opened the doors, the hood, the rear trunk hatch. Even the glove compartment. I had to touch everything! I felt the wood, the seats, the carpet. I couldn't get enough of it. And it shines like a new penny.

"It is exactly the right color!"

I was being louder than I usually am, but I couldn't control it. I was overwhelmed by what Norm and his men had done with those decrepit pieces we brought back from Salt Lake.

Where Norm found wide whitewall tires for it, I'll never know, but I sure am glad he did.

"It has the original flathead V-8 and all the original running gear. We rebuilt everything. You didn't know it, but Samuel is an upholsterer." Norm said.

Norm stopped and pointed to Samuel, 'Sam', and waved at him to come over to us.

Norm put his arm around him and acted like he was his own son.

"He did all the seats, carpet, side panels and the roof." Norm said. "He even put insulation in the doors and side panels."

Sam turned toward me and I shook his hand and he stood with us as Norm went on about the wonders of the Woody.

"All the numbers match. This is exactly the way it looked when it came off the production line in 1941." He said. "I've already had an offer of fifty thousand for it." Norm said.

While Jim and I were looking and listening to Norm, everyone from the office showed up with food. Tables and chairs got set up and suddenly there was a party going on that they had planned. I heard some talk and they all knew about the Woody.

Later I found out that Norm had them all come to his shop after he finished the car a few weeks ago. Denise called Norm after I called her. They set up this big party for us that day.

Jim was overwhelmed too. His favorite girlfriend was there with hugs and kisses. I know Jim has bought a ring and is planning to propose to her.

What I don't know is when this is supposed to happen. But we'll have a party then too.

Jim and I and the women were sitting in the back when Lieutenant Lopez came over to us. We talked for quite a while when he mentioned his father.

"Dad would be surprised at what we have done in the past few years." He said.

"What did your dad do for a living?"

"Unlike most of the people around here who are ranchers, he was a farmer. We lived south and east of here where we had some water." Lopez said.

I just got an ornery thought. "Well then. Do you think that we could call you 'Farmer Brown'"? I asked in my most sincere voice and coy smile.

"Not even for a second!" He said and glared at me.

We all laughed for a long time about that. But it will be forgotten by tomorrow. I promise!

We didn't get much work done, but we talked about work all day. I didn't get to crash on the couch till hours later but Denise was there to help me get rid of all my aches and pains.